Peculiarities at the Picnic

MISS MARKHAM MYSTERY SERIES
BOOK TWO

JULIET E. SIDONIE

Peculiarities at the Picnic

MISS MARKHAM MYSTERY SERIES
BOOK TWO

JULIET E. SIDONIE

Murder Among Friends—A Miss Markham Mystery

ISBN 978-1-7330444-3-1 (hardcover) — 978-1-7330444-4-8 (paperback)

Copyright © 2025 by Miss Markham Mysteries, LLC

All rights reserved. Neither this book, nor any parts within it may be sold or reproduced in any form or by any electronic or mechanical means, including information storage and retrieval systems without permission in writing from the author. The only exception is by a reviewer, who may quote short excerpts in a review.

This is a work of fiction. Though some characters are inspired by real life historical figures, this book is the product of the authors' imagination, and the work is entirely fictional in nature. In all other respects, any resemblance to actual persons, living or dead, places, or actual events is purely coincidental, except where permission has been given to use real names. The incidents, dialogue, and situations described within this work are fictional and not be construed as real. The views and opinions expressed in this book are solely those of the authors and do not reflect the views or opinions of the publisher.

This book is dedicated to Jim Duly—Mr. Jameson—without whom the Jameson Picnic wouldn't be up and running today. It is also dedicated to Doris Markham, our inspiration and role model for Miss Deloris Markham.

Acknowledgments

We would like to thank our families for their support, suggestions and help. Thanks especially go to Elden Dilks, Kristie Zorn, Patty Baker, Jim and Jan Duly, Craig Blocksome, Bill and Pat Swinney, Dan Mason, Nancy McCrary, Shane Roberts, and Pat Hightree. Your help, feedback and permissions were extremely helpful in writing this book. Thank you to Sara McClure, Rebecca Blocksome, and Lenora Dilks for your expertise in formatting, editing, and artwork. Thank you also to our Beta Readers, Joyce Henkins, Gail Metcalf-Schartel, Racheal Shatswell, Judy Pellitier, Rosie Russell, Jo Ann Day, Jan Duly, Annie Wheeler, and Patty Baker for your feedback, suggestions, and especially for catching errors. One final thank you to Trudi Burton at the Daviess County Historical Society and the Jameson Community Betterment Association for their permission to print the map.

MORE INFORMATION

At the back of the book, you will find a sneak peek at our next book. Visit our website at MissMarkhamMysteries.com for more information.

Table of Contents

Foreword — xi
List of Characters — xiii
Map of Jameson — xix

Prologue — 1
1. Letters From Home — 7
2. Time Off — 15
3. Home — 23
4. Investigation — 29
5. The Picnic — 37
6. Main Street — 43
7. Back to the Picnic — 53
8. Back to Main Street — 59
9. The Talent Show — 69
10. Sarah Hawkins Green Gibbs — 75
11. Bert's Theory — 83
12. Bart and Corny — 89
13. Friday Night at the Picnic — 95
14. The Dance — 101
15. The Back Roads — 107
16. The Parade — 115
17. Finders Keepers — 121
18. Lucinda — 125
19. Clifford Candy — 135
20. Cathy Narramore — 141
21. Picnic-Goers — 147
22. The Sheriff — 157
23. The Drawing — 165
24. Sunday Dinner — 169
25. The Narramores — 173
26. Town Meeting — 179

Epilogue	191
About the Author(s)	195
Miss Markham Mysteries	197
Prologue	199

Foreword

In 1936, a fire ravaged the peaceful town of Jameson, Missouri, destroying almost the entire downtown on Main Street. The inhabitants picked up the pieces and rebuilt two buildings out of the bricks left behind: Duly's Garage and the vacant building to the north. *Deadly Peculiarities at the Picnic* takes place in August 1931, before the disastrous fire occurred, when the town was a bustling center of activities. If you visit Jameson today, you won't be able to see the downtown as Miss Markham saw it in 1931; however, the annual Jameson Picnic continues to be held in August each year in the City Park. It doesn't have the carnival rides or games, but it still has the baby show and its famous tenderloins and homemade pies. I just learned that the cookshack is now torn down and a new one will be built in 2025.

List of Characters

~ DAVIESS COUNTY RESIDENTS ~

Alfia "Alfie" Thompson—a childhood friend of Deloris. Her family owns Thompson's General Store.

Amos Conaway—Lucinda's boyfriend in 1917 who died in the Great War (now known as World War I).

Bartholomew "Bart" Shaw—one of Emmett "Old Man" Jones' laborers. He drives an old jalopy that is notoriously unreliable, unrepaired, and just plain ugly.

Cornelius "Corny" Higgins—another of Emmett "Old Man" Jones' laborers. Everyone called him Corny partly because of his name and partly because of the quality of jokes he tells.

Craig Ness—a local farmer who is the proud owner of a brand-new tractor.

Emmett "Old Man" Jones—Jameson's finest busybody. Emmett is known throughout Daviess County for his excellent skills as a builder, and even better skills at knowing all the latest gossip.

Gary Green—disappeared fourteen years ago in 1917. A man with an unsavory reputation whom no one missed very much.

Geoffrey and Moira Harvey—president of the Jameson Farmers Bank and his wife. Moira is a British immigrant and the proprietor of a tea and coffee shop in Jameson.

Lara Cogswell—a recently retired schoolmistress who never married. She lives comfortably on an inheritance from her parents, which includes the family home.

Liam O'Casey—went steady with Deloris in high school, before she broke it off and moved to Kansas City. He moved to Saint Joseph, but now he is back in town for the picnic and to visit his uncle, Sean O'Casey.

Lucinda "Cindy" Hawkins—Gary Green's sixteen-year-old stepdaughter, who disappeared at the same time as him in 1917.

Oliver Gibbs—the hired hand on the Green farm. Sarah hired him right after Gary Green disappeared.

Owen and Nellie Robertson—owners of the Robertson Mercantile and Millinery store in town.

Sarah Hawkins Green-Gibbs—farmer who married Gary Green after the death of her first husband, Jethro Hawkins. She has one child, a daughter, Lucinda, whom she calls Cindy, from her marriage to Jethro.

Frankie Martin—the telephone operator for Jameson.

Sean O'Casey—generally a grumpy curmudgeon and proud of it. His farm and barn are on the north edge of town. A row of trees divides his barn and beanfield from the city park where the picnic is held. His house is across the road from the beanfield.

Silas and Cathy (Willis) Narramore—high school friend of Lucinda "Cindy" Hawkins and her husband.

Tom and Maude Fine—the Mayor of Jameson and his wife.

~ KANSAS CITY RESIDENTS ~

Austin Martin—son of Frankie Martin and a childhood friend of Deloris. A detective with the Kansas City Police Department who also came home to Jameson for the annual picnic.

Les Wells—a cute boy about Deloris' age from Independence, Missouri, who she met at the picnic; he was perfectly happy to flirt with her.

Marguerite Adcock—a childhood friend of Thelma Webb during their time together at the Jameson Elementary School, now married and living in Kansas City. Her house was robbed a few months before, and Deloris helped solve the crime.

~ MARKHAM FAMILY ~

Clarence Markham—Deloris' older brother, who lives and works on the family farm.

Clifford Candy—hired hand for the Markham family who lives next door.

Deloris "DeDe" Markham—a brunette with violet eyes, a knockout figure, and good-looking gams. She loves to investigate mysteries and doesn't mind telling a fib or two in order to accomplish her ends.

Mildred and Berniece Markham—cousins to Deloris. They were orphaned at an early age and taken in by their Aunt Nan Markham. They lived on the Markham farm until adulthood.

Nannie Markham—the matriarch of the Markham family. She cares for everyone in the family, but she also holds very strong views on appropriate and polite behavior, from which her family often strays.

Roy and Bert Markham—oldest brother- and sister-in-law to Deloris. They live on their own farm between Jameson and Gallatin in rural Daviess County. Bert loves to know what's going on and is happy to share all the news and gossip she learns.

Thelma Webb—Deloris' twice-divorced older sister who is raising two children on her own in Kansas City. To help make ends meet, she rents rooms in her house to single female boarders like Gracie Burnett.

Will Markham—the patriarch of the Markham family, who loves his wife dearly but occasionally deviates from her views on what is proper behavior.

Map of Jameson

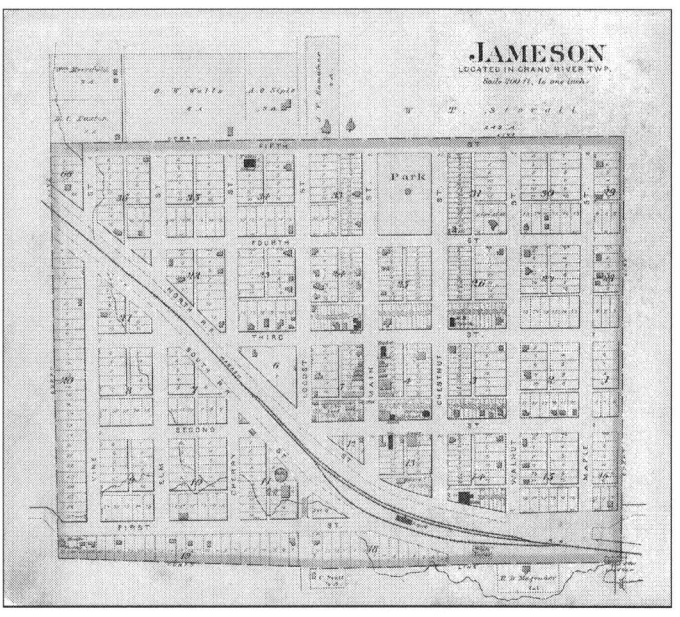

Prologue
THE BANDSTAND

It was never a good sign when the sky turned dark on a summer afternoon in Northwest Missouri, Maude Fine thought, looking warily upwards. As she kept watch, the clouds changed from white fluff balls to gray rain clouds, and then into a dark green, angry, swirling mass as evening arrived early. Into the eerie stillness, as the birds stopped singing, a sound like thunder emerged, growing louder and louder until it sounded like a train roaring in towards the depot. But no train was due, and the residents of Jameson, like Maude, knew what that sound was as they hurried to take shelter. A tornado was coming and by the sound of it, a bad one.

Playing a giant game of hopscotch, the tornado touched down, lifted up, and touched down again to the accompaniment of moaning winds and cracking trees. Eventually, the storm and its destruction moved on and the night became peaceful.

Early the next morning, Maude and her husband, Jameson's mayor Tom Fine, went for a drive to see what the destructive storm had done as it danced around twisting and turning through the town. They weren't the only ones keen to survey the damage; the residents of Jameson were out in full force to clear trees and take stock of what also needed to be repaired. Luckily, most of the tornado's damage had been in the fields north of town, with the houses in Jameson spared with a few missing shingles and broken windows.

Tom and Maude pulled to a stop by City Park, where the bandstand roof took a direct hit from a falling oak tree and collapsed completely.

"There's no fixing that," Maude said.

"No," her husband shook his head, "it'll have to be rebuilt."

Maude waved as Nellie and Owen Robertson approached from the other direction on Chestnut Street. Owen stopped his vehicle across from the Fines' car and leaned out of his window. Tom did the same and Nellie leaned across Owen towards the open window.

"Can you get the bandstand put up again in time?" Nellie asked Tom. "The picnic is only five weeks away."

"I reckon so," Tom replied. "I'm going to call Old Man Jones to see what can be done."

"Good," Nellie said. "If anyone can get it built in time, he can."

"Just tell Old Man Jones to build it as quickly as he talks," Maude said to her husband, with a twinkle in her eye. "It'll be up in no time."

Later that morning, Emmett "Old Man" Jones pulled into the city park in his 1926 Model TT Ford pickup with his dog Rex sitting on the seat beside him, sniffing the air through the rolled-down window. Old Man Jones was well-known throughout Daviess County for the quality of his construction work and the quantity of his words. The mayor was waiting for him, and the two men walked over to the bandstand.

"Can you rebuild it before the picnic?" Tom asked.

"Don't you worry none," Emmett replied. "The Jameson Picnic has been meeting on or close to August 9th for the past thirty-nine years and I don't aim to let one little tornado stop it now."

"Good," the mayor said, looking relieved. "The picnic wouldn't be the same without it."

"Bart and Corny are on their way," Emmett continued. "I had them stop at the lumberyard to place an order for what we'll need. The planks for the stage and the roof should be easy enough to get, but I wasn't sure if they'd have them big timbers we needed for the supports. And everybody's out buying those asbestos shingles today, thanks to that dern storm. We won't need 'em until we get the rest of the bandstand built, but I wanted to git our order in to make sure they'd have 'em when we need 'em." Emmett gestured towards the wreckage of the tree and the bandstand. "We'll have all this mess taken out before sundown or my name ain't Emmett Meriweather Jones. Should be able to start rebuilding tomorrow, iffen one of the hardware stores in this here town has got everything else we need. An' iffen they don't, I'll send Bart and Corny over to Pattonsburg or Coffey. That is, if Bart's old jalopy don't break down. That car is held together by bailing twine and bull—" Emmett stopped abruptly, remembering who he was talking to.

"I'll tell everyone the picnic will go ahead as scheduled," the mayor said, trying to find a way to end the conversation.

"Yessir," Emmett said. "I'll get a new bandstand up lickety-split, ready for the talent show and baby contest, baking contest, an' all the bands—plus the place for you to speak from, of course." He licked his lips at the memory of past picnics when he entered the pie-eating and watermelon-eating contests and then ate a tenderloin followed with more homemade pie. "No siree, can't have the picnic without the bandstand," he continued, "but it's an easy job. No need to install windows or walls, just rebuild the stage and put a roof over it to block the sun. Nothing to gum up the works."

Emmett pointed to another building ten feet away. "And the tree didn't even take out the cookshack. That woulda been a bigger job, what with the kitchen equipment and all. I'm just glad I caught Craig Ness at his farm 'fore I come over here. He should be here soon."

"Why is Craig coming?" the mayor asked, interested despite himself.

"Didn't ya hear? He just bought hisself a new Farmall F30 tractor from over in Gallatin. It's still shiny an' everything. That oak tree ain't an acorn, you know? Figure we can pull it away with the tractor faster'n trying to saw it up into pieces to move. You should hear that engine go—it's got enough power to pull anything. I brought chains to attach the tree to the tractor; they're in the back of my truck. Craig's gonna pull the tree down the road to O'Casey's barn and cut it up fer firewood there. O'Casey is an ol' devil, but I talked him into letting us move everything over there since his barn is close." Old Man Jones gave a toothy grin and continued, "I told him the entire citizenry of Jameson would be lathered up at him iffen he didn't. He don't want to get on the bad side of them old biddies in town. Meaning no disrespect to your missus, Mayor, but them ladies can be a might scary when they get riled. And we'll move what's left of the old bandstand there, too, and whoever wants the scraps can pick 'em up themselves. Then—"

Rex interrupted the conversation, barking from the pickup at the rumbling arrival of Craig Ness on his tractor. Jones stopped talking for a second to wave at Craig, and, seizing his chance, the mayor quickly said, "I'll leave everything in your hands. Good day, Emmett." He offered a handshake and then walked away, while Old Man Jones started talking to Craig about the finer points of the new tractor.

Bart and Corny arrived with a rattle and a backfire in a dusty old jalopy just as Craig's tractor made short work of hauling away the tree. Once the tree was gone, it was time to start removing the debris from the bandstand. Rex, who had been tied up and kept inside the pickup so that he wouldn't be underfoot while the tractor was working, leaped out as soon as Emmett untied him and opened the door. The dog relieved himself as soon as his feet touched the ground and then ran over to greet Bart and Corny where they stood, looking at the squashed roof of the bandstand. Once there, however, the hound seemed to abandon his greeting, and instead started sniffing determinedly.

"You smell somethin', boy?" Emmett asked.

"Prob'ly just a ground squirrel or rabbit," Bart opined.

Rex picked up a trail and followed it to the far edge of the destroyed bandstand where the floor had come up, pulling with it the posts that had secured the bandstand into the earth for thirty-nine years. Rex began rooting through the boards and debris with his nose and paws. He used his jaws to pick up a board and move it to one side and then another. Eventually, he got to the bottom of the destruction to bare ground and began digging.

"Fool dog," Emmett said fondly. "We got to get to work, Rex, and you don't need no rabbit or bone."

Emmett went over to pull the dog away from his quest

so that they could start work. Just as he reached down to grab the rope he used as a collar on the dog, he stopped. There at Rex's feet were bones all right, in the shape of a human hand.

"Tarnation!" was the only word coming from his mouth. For the first time in his life, Old Man Jones was left speechless.

"What the ...?" was the only response Corny managed to get out when he walked over and saw the cream-colored bones resting in the shallow depression Rex had dug.

"Boss, is that a hand?" Bart asked.

Emmett Jones nodded, still unable to speak.

"Runned over to Frankie Martin's house an' call the sheriff," Emmett told Bart, finally finding his voice. "I'm gonna stay here with Corny and make sure ol' Rex don't disturb nothing else."

Bart nodded in reply, but then he stopped and asked, "Ain't Miz Martin in that new telephone building?"

"Oh, dern it, yes, I mean go to the telephone building and ask her to call the sheriff. I fergit she just moved in there last week. Now git." Then Old Man Jones looked at Corny and added, "Put Rex back in the truck and tie him up, he don't need to do no more digging today."

CHAPTER 1
Letters From Home

When Deloris Markham arrived back at her sister's boarding house after her Thursday morning shift as an operator at the police switchboard, there were two letters and a newspaper waiting for her. She normally would have read the letters first, as the newspaper from her hometown tended towards exciting stories like the price of corn, the weather, and who had relatives visiting from Buckner, Independence or Sibley, Missouri. Today, though, the headline from *The Jameson Gem* caught her eye. In large, bold type normally reserved for national news headlines, it read,

BODY AT THE BANDSTAND

"Thelma," Deloris called out to her older sister, "have you seen this?"

"What's that?" Thelma replied as she poked her head out of the kitchen.

"Have you seen this?" Deloris repeated as she pointed to the headlines of *The Jameson Gem*.

Thelma walked into the living room to see and collapsed on the sofa next to Deloris. The two sisters sat there dumbfounded, each staring at the headline. Then Deloris started to read the article out loud.

"The remains of Gary Green were found last Thursday when workers arrived to clean up the tornado damage to the bandstand on the Jameson Park grounds. Identification was made based upon a driver's license found in a wallet on the remains and a pocket watch laying beside the deceased. No money was found in the wallet, leading the sheriff to believe he may have been robbed before being murdered. Gary Green disappeared fourteen years ago when it was believed he left the county in the company of his stepdaughter, Lucinda Hawkins, for parts unknown."

"Oh my," Thelma exclaimed when Deloris paused from reading the article. "Mr. Green wasn't a nice man, but I didn't think anyone would kill him for it."

"You knew him?"

"Well, I knew *of* him, let's say. Lucinda, or Cindy, as we called her, was in my class when we were at Big Creek School and we were friends up until I left after eighth grade. I lost contact with her when I had to drop out of school to help Momma take care of you and our cousins, Mildred and Berniece. She went on to Jameson High School and would have graduated from there if she hadn't disappeared in her junior year. She, Cathy Willis, Marguerite Adcock and I were all in the same grade and such good friends." Thelma smiled at the memory of her. "She was the sweetest girl with the prettiest golden colored hair and big blue eyes. All the boys who rode our school wagon had a crush on her."

Deloris continued reading the article, *"With the discovery of his remains, suspicion now falls upon his wife,*

Sarah Hawkins Green, and her daughter, Lucinda Hawkins. More details with be forthcoming."

"Oh, that can't be right," Thelma responded. "Cindy and Mrs. Green wouldn't have hurt him. They were both afraid of him, but Cindy wouldn't even kill a bug. She was so kind to the younger children on the school wagon and even shared her blanket with little Myrtle Saunders, wrapping her up in it when the wood stove went out on the wagon."

"Well, somebody didn't like him enough to kill him!" Deloris exclaimed.

Thelma added, "As I said, he wasn't a nice man and I can see him making someone mad enough, but..." her voice trailed off as the memory of him returned to her mind and she gave a shudder. She stood and walked into the kitchen in deep thought.

Deloris re-read the article; her mind was going as fast as a train. Who would kill anyone in Jameson and bury a body there? Things like this just didn't happen in her hometown. Deloris then turned to the two letters waiting on her lap. She chose the one from her Momma, Nannie Markham, first.

Deloris opened the letter with trepidation. She loved her Momma, but Nannie Markham had no qualms about letting her children know if she was disappointed in their actions. Nannie started it by announcing the murder, but she never liked to gossip, so she said basically nothing different from what was in the newspaper. Then she wrote about which family members came to visit last Sunday and who was at church. Deloris knew that the reference to family visiting was a hint that she and Thelma hadn't been home in a while. A flicker of guilt crossed her mind. Mission accomplished, Momma, she thought to herself with a slight shake of her head.

Reading on, her mother then discussed the garden and how she was starting to get so many tomatoes, onions, and peppers that she needed to start canning them. *"The green beans should be ready to pick in a week or so and the corn is coming on nicely, if the weather would cooperate. The calf that the old yeller cow had in February got its head stuck in the fence and your Dad had to really work to get it untangled, what with all the vines climbing up the fence. He came back with poison ivy on his arms and after he washed up, I had to lather him down with calamine lotion. Are you, Thelma and the girls planning to come up for the Jameson Picnic? It's August 6th, 7th & 8th. Mildred and Berniece are putting their babies in the baby show. Let me know if you and Thelma are coming so that I can get your beds ready. Write Soon. Love, Momma."*

When Thelma came back out of the kitchen, Deloris asked her, "Are you going up home for the Jameson Picnic this year?"

"I don't know. When is it?"

"Momma says it is August 6th, 7th and 8th."

"I'll need to see if I can take off from the diner that Friday," Thelma replied, "and let Albert know I'm not available for dinner that weekend."

"I'm sure your new boyfriend will miss you horribly. You could take him with you to Jameson," Deloris said with a mischievous grin.

"And have Momma, Dad, Roy, and Clarence all try to interrogate him?" Thelma giggled. "I'll wait for a few months before I introduce him to the family."

"I'll need to see if I can take off from Poppy's Paradise

PECULIARITIES AT THE PICNIC

Park," Deloris mused. "But I want to go up earlier than Friday."

Deloris then turned to the second letter. It was from Bert, Deloris' and Thelma's sister-in-law, who was married to their brother, Roy Markham. Bert included a newspaper clipping from the Gallatin newspaper with her thick ten-page letter. Deloris read her letter out loud to Thelma who began sewing.

Bert started by providing the same information as Nannie, but then her letter went on to give more local gossip. The Gallatin paper clipping gave a different spin on the story, saying there were no suspects yet.

Bert wrote, *"I remember hearing rumors about the Greens and how awful Gary Green treated his wife and stepdaughter. I felt so sorry for them, especially Sarah Green. She lost her first husband, Lucinda's father, when he was kicked in the head by one of their mules. Then her daughter disappeared, along with her second husband. Shortly after Gary disappeared, she hired Oliver Gibbs to help her take care of the farm and the farm animals. Sarah never remarried after that, and she always looked so sad. This is one more tragedy for her.*

"Gary disappeared fourteen years ago, but I remember it like it was yesterday. I heard about him even in Pattonsburg. Everyone thought that he either kidnapped Lucinda, killed her, or that she willingly ran away with him—which I doubt very much. We honestly were afraid that we would find her body instead of his and, who knows, we may still find her body one day. What a shock to find out that he has been dead all this time.

"The town is all abuzz with theories and rumors now, and the matrons of the town are in a tizzy. Neighbors are

looking at neighbors suspiciously, accusing each other of having a personal vendetta to even the score with Gary.

"People also say that Lucinda must have murdered Gary and ran away to avoid getting caught. It looks like Lucinda either was murdered or did run away because no one has heard from her during this time—not even her mother.

"They are also looking suspiciously at Sarah, because others believe she must have murdered him to stop him from abusing her and to protect her daughter. Then she must have sent Lucinda away, or Lucinda ran away when she saw what her mother had done. Sarah couldn't run because she had the farm to tend to, and that is why she hired Oliver Gibbs to help her. He does odd jobs around the farm, repairing fences, fixing the barn door and running errands. When Sarah and Oliver come to town, people don't say a word to her or him. They just move away from her and then stop and stare before they start whispering about them having an affair—like they know what goes on in their lives.

"Gary didn't have many friends, but his one friend, Corny Higgins, is the one going around accusing Sarah. I just can't believe she had anything to do with any of it. One look at her face and you can see the pain and suffering she has endured."

Then Bert changed the subject talking about Roy, the family, their farm, the crops, and the weather. She ended with the question, *"Are you guys coming up for the picnic? Deloris, since you solved Marguerite Adcock's mystery, maybe you could also solve this murder mystery? You can come up for the picnic and enter the Talent Show and it can be your talent. Haha."*

Deloris paused and looked up at Thelma. "Say, have you heard from Marguerite since the robbery in June?"

"No, I've been meaning to call her and see how she is

doing. Her baby is due any day now," Thelma replied. "I'm not sure Bert should encourage you like that."

"I did solve her robbery. And the murder at Poppy's Paradise Park."

"True, but do you think Momma would approve of you investigating in Jameson?" Deloris shrugged, but they both knew that Momma would most certainly not approve. "What else does Bert say?"

Not much, just finishing with: *"Seriously, I really miss seeing you and Thelma. Roy does too. Love, Bert."*

There it was. Even though she had a job in Kansas City, Deloris had to find a way to get to the picnic this year, to see her family and try to help Mrs. Green out of this mess. Deloris remembered seeing Mrs. Green in town and she'd felt sorry for her, too. When she saw her, she always smiled and said hello to her. Mrs. Green would smile back, but her smile never seemed to reach her eyes. Deloris had already solved a murder at the amusement park where she worked. If she could solve one in Kansas City, then surely she could solve one in her hometown.

Besides, for Deloris, the picnic ranked equally with her birthday and Christmas as one of her favorite times of the year. She tried to never miss a picnic and so far, in her eighteen—almost nineteen—years of existence, her attendance had been stellar. The picnic had a certain mystical draw with its lights, music, amusement rides, cotton candy, tenderloins, free drawing, games, the baby show, and seeing friends and family. But now she was an adult, with a job where she worked on the weekends. She didn't know if she could make it back, but she was going to try.

Her thoughts of the picnic were interrupted with Thelma announcing that lunch was ready, and Deloris needed to "Wash up and tell the others."

CHAPTER 2

Time Off

Deloris worked two jobs because finding a full-time job since the depression started in 1929 was almost impossible. One job was the switchboard at the Kansas City, Missouri Police Department where she worked Monday through Friday in the mornings, and the other was at Poppy's Paradise Park's soda fountain, where she worked Friday and Saturday nights and Sunday afternoons.

When she went to work at the switchboard on Friday for her morning shift, Deloris asked her supervisor, Mary Virginia, if she could take off on Thursday and Friday, August 6th and 7th. The picnic was Thursday to Saturday but she didn't work at the switchboard on Saturday, so she only needed those two days off. Mary Virginia told her she could take off as long as she found someone else to work for her. With only two weeks to find someone, Deloris went to work on it immediately.

When she got home that afternoon, she knocked on the bedroom door of her friend and fellow boarder in Thelma's house, Gracie Burnett, who worked the weekend day shift on the switchboard.

"Hey Gracie, do you think you could cover the switchboard for me on August 6th and 7th in the morning?"

"I don't know. Let me look at my calendar." Gracie turned to the calendar hanging on her wall and said, "Oh, sorry Deloris, I can't. I have an appointment Thursday morning with my advisor at school to get registered for the fall semester classes and the next day I have an orientation in the chemistry lab with my chemistry teacher. I'd help you if I could."

Gracie was attending the newly chartered University of Kansas City and studying to be a coroner. Deloris had heard talk about the new university that was in the process of acquiring buildings and acreage.

"Hey, why don't you ask Abby?" Gracie offered.

At Deloris' puzzled look, Gracie clarified, "Abigail Singleton. I guess you haven't met her yet. She just started working weekends on the switchboard with me a couple of weeks ago and is looking to pick up some extra cash."

"All right. How do I find Abby?"

"Her telephone number is Jefferson 1-531. She and I made plans to go out on the town this Saturday and I got her number to complete our plans," Gracie said, pleased that she could help Deloris.

"Thanks," Deloris said, and she went downstairs to the telephone in the hall. She picked up the earpiece from the phone in the hallway and clicked the receiver hook twice to notify the operator that she wanted to place a call. Then she gave the operator Abby's number to dial.

When someone picked up on the other end, Deloris said cheerfully, "Hello, is this Abby Singleton? Oh, she doesn't know me, but tell her I am a friend of Gracie Burnett. Yes, I'll wait."

A minute later, Abby answered, "Hello."

"Hello Abby, my name is Deloris Markham and I am a friend of Gracie Burnett. I work at the police switchboard during the week in the mornings and I need to find someone to cover for me on Thursday and Friday morning, August 6th and 7th." Deloris grinned at Abby's response. "You will? Gee, that's swell! I'll tell Mary Virginia to expect you those two days. Thanks a lot!"

Beaming, Deloris hung up the phone and went back upstairs to tell Gracie that Abby was going to work for her. "Thank you for suggesting her to me."

"Not a problem at all. Hey, what are you going to do on those two days?"

Deloris didn't see a need to tell Gracie about her ulterior motive to investigate a fourteen-year-old murder, so she simply said, "Well, I am really going to be gone for four and a half days. I'm taking the train up to Jameson on Wednesday night to attend my hometown gathering on Thursday, Friday, and Saturday, and then return on Sunday."

That night, at Poppy's Paradise Park, she planned to approach Mr. Pat O'Brien, her direct supervisor there, to ask about taking off the of August 7th, 8th and 9th. She worked Fridays, Saturdays, and Sundays at the park, so she didn't need to ask for Thursday off. It could be confusing working two jobs with different days and hours. She realized that weekend would probably be a very busy at Poppy's Paradise Park, but she'd earned the time off. For the past month, she had been working a double shift to cover until someone could be hired to work the soda fountain shift another employee had worked. A few days ago, Mr. O'Brien finally hired a guy, but she didn't feel right asking the new guy to cover for her since he had been a little slow on the learning process.

Deloris arrived at the amusement park early, and before she went to the locker room to change into her uniform, she knocked on the door to Mr. O'Brien's office. He looked up from working on the payroll and smiled when he saw it was Deloris. Waving her to come in, he said, "What can I do for you, young lady?"

"I need to take the weekend of August 7th, 8th and 9th off," she said matter-of-factly.

"Oh, I see. I hope there isn't anything wrong with your family?" A worried look replaced the smile.

"It's my hometown gathering and my family is expecting me to be there, especially my mother. She needs me to help her with her baking preparations," Deloris said, looking at the pencil holder on his desk and crossing her fingers behind her back. It was only a small white lie. Her mother was expecting her, but didn't need her help with anything—Momma was quite capable of baking the pies she was asked to donate without Deloris.

"Well, I know how mothers can be persistent. Let me see. That is the weekend before the Ararat Shriners' Picnic. I couldn't possibly let you take that weekend off, but since it is the week before, I just need you to find someone to cover for you. I suppose you could use a break. I do appreciate all your help covering the extra shifts at the soda fountain these last few weeks."

"Thank you, Mr. O'Brien," Deloris said, and she quickly turned and hustled through his door before he could change his mind.

In the locker room before her shift, Deloris approached Gloria to ask her to cover for her. Gloria didn't really like

Deloris and flat out told her no. Then she turned her back to Deloris to continue putting on her uniform. That was really no big surprise to Deloris, but she thought she would ask her, anyway. Miracles do happen once in a while.

Next, Trudie walked into the locker room to change, and Deloris asked her. She usually worked between the beer garden and the concession stand, but lately she had been helping Deloris in the soda fountain until a replacement could be hired. Trudie worked hard to support herself, her mother and her young daughter since her husband left her. She readily agreed to help Deloris; besides, it gave her a little extra in her paycheck and that never hurt.

"Sure, honey. I can cover for you. Whatcha got going on? Another murder you need to solve?"

Deloris gasped, "How'd you guess?"

"Ha, well, I was only joking, but it figures you'd be involved in something like that."

"Well, it's actually for a hometown reunion type of event, but, yes, there has been a murder, too. I feel like I need to help make sure they arrest the guilty person or persons and not hang it on the widow's neck or her daughter's."

"Oh hey, I just remembered something. I can't cover for you that Sunday," Trudie said apologetically. "That's my daughter's first communion and my mother has a big dinner planned."

"That's okay, Trudie. I'll see if Stella can cover that day for me."

As luck would have it, Stella walked in at that moment and raised an eyebrow when she heard her name. Deloris explained the situation and Stella readily agreed to work that Sunday for Deloris.

"You are the bee's knees! I really want to thank you for covering for me."

"That's okay. I'm happy to help you. I know that you have had to work a lot of hours since..." Stella said and then became a little choked up. "You know."

"Yes, I know, Stella. Even though he could be frustrating at times, we all miss him," Deloris said as she put a consoling arm around Stella's shoulders. She had always suspicioned that Stella had a little crush on their friend who was murdered at Poppy's a few weeks before.

Deloris took a moment to think about that whole experience. After she'd solved the intertwined mystery of Marguerite's robbery and a murder at the park, she'd wondered if she'd ever get the chance to do more detecting. She enjoyed investigating the mysteries and bringing the culprits to justice. Life had seemed a little dull since then, and she was happy to have another mystery to solve.

As Deloris walked to the soda fountain to begin her shift, she thought to herself, "Thank goodness I was able to get people to cover for me. That was the hard part. Now I get to start my investigation and look a little deeper into the murder and circumstances surrounding it."

The day was sweltering hot, and the crowd at the soda fountain was swelling by the minute. Mr. O'Brien, checking in, saw that it was at capacity and called Stella in to help Deloris keep up.

Between orders, Deloris told Stella all about the letters and newspapers from Jameson.

The next morning, before she left for her double shift at Poppy's, Deloris sketched a plan in her notebook of what she wanted to accomplish up home and questions to ask folks. Even though she wouldn't be leaving for a few days, she started to pack. When she told Thema that she would

PECULIARITIES AT THE PICNIC

leave Wednesday afternoon, Thelma asked her to take some apple butter she'd made up to Momma, and Deloris agreed.

The rest of the weekend went quickly, as Deloris worked double shifts both days and continued training the new guy at the soda fountain.

On Monday, after her shift at the police switchboard ended, Deloris went downstairs to the main floor of the police station to talk with her friend, Austin Martin. She'd known Austin all her life, as their parents had been friends since before she was born. Austin graduated a year earlier than Deloris from Jameson High School, and immediately after graduating, he moved to Kansas City and joined the police force. He did so well that he was already a junior detective, and Chief Denton recommended him for a fast-track promotion to full detective, in part because of his role in solving the murder of Deloris' coworker.

Deloris wanted to ask Austin if he was going to go back to Jameson for the picnic. She knew Thelma wanted to go, but couldn't afford bus or train tickets for herself and her daughters. She also suspected he might not like the idea of her poking around into Gary Green's death.

"Hey, DeDe. How's tricks?" Austin asked as she walked over to his desk.

DeDe was a nickname Deloris had since she was a child with a stuttering problem and couldn't say her own name. Only her family and close friends called her DeDe.

"Hey, Austin. Did you see the news from up home about the body they found under the bandstand?"

"Yes, why?" He eyed her suspiciously.

"I'm planning to go up early and see if I can help the local authorities."

"DeDe," he admonished. "Stay out of their investigation."

"But I know I can help. People will talk to me when they might not talk to the sheriff."

"DeDe ..." Austin rubbed his forehead in frustration.

"Are you going up to the picnic?" she cunningly changed the subject.

Austin let his hand drop to his desk and sighed, "I plan to be up there on Friday."

"Are you driving up?" she asked. Austin nodded. "Would you like some company? Thelma doesn't want to miss work, so she can't come as early as me, but I know she'd love to be there."

"Sure," Austin smiled. "I'd be happy to take Thelma and the girls as long as she can leave Friday afternoon and we can drive back on Sunday after lunch."

"Great! You're the best!" Deloris said. "I'll tell Thelma when I get home."

Deloris jumped up from her seat and headed home. When Thelma got home from her shift at Leed's Lunch Counter, she told her about the offer from Austin. Thelma was overjoyed to accept, and she, like Deloris, busied herself with packing for the trip up home.

CHAPTER 3
Home

On Wednesday afternoon, Deloris' older brother, Clarence, met her at the Jameson train station. "How was the trip?" he asked.

"We were squished in like sardines," Deloris said with a smile. "Seems like every year there's more people who come to the picnic."

"Every year more folks move away," Clarence asserted, "to darn fool places like Kansas City." Deloris stuck her tongue out at her brother, who grinned. "Here, DeDe, give me your luggage."

Clarence put her suitcase in the rumble seat and then hopped in on the driver's side of the black 1926 Model T Runabout. Deloris put her other smaller bag at her feet. She grabbed the flashlight from the bag and started rifling through its contents. It held a couple of pencils, plus a flashlight, a rope, and various other items in case she needed them in her investigation. Just as she feared, she left her notebook in Kansas City. "I'll just use my old Big Chief."

"What?" Clarence asked.

"Oh nothing, I just realized that I forgot to bring something." She would need to write down what she sketched in her notebook as soon as she arrived home.

As they drove away from the train station, Deloris asked Clarence about the repairs to the bandstand and if the Knights of Pythias, who organized the picnic, had completed all the preparations. Clarence told her that as promised, Emmett Jones and his workers got the bandstand replaced in time for the picnic, but not without a hiccup or two. They had to wait until the sheriff finished his investigation and released the crime scene for them to get back to work. With the two-week delay, they had to work fast with long hours, and Old Man Jones had to relent and hire another hand to help get the work done. Two days before the picnic, it stood ready with its new floor, new stairs, and new roof. It was bigger than the old one, with more room to accommodate the baby show and bigger bands.

He explained that throughout the process, the women in town brought the workers lunch and supper so that they wouldn't have to leave the grounds. "I heard Corny say that he wished it wasn't over so soon, because that was the best eating he had ever done," Clarence said with a chuckle.

"That sounds like Corny," Deloris said, laughing.

On the Monday before the picnic, Clarence continued, the Knights of Pythias, of which their father, Will Markham, was a member, had their last meeting to finalize their plans for the picnic. The members' wives, including their mother, Nannie Markham, belonged to the Pythian Sisters, who met the same night at Harvey's Tea and Coffee Shop. The Sisters planned the food and work schedules for the cookshack, leaving the men to arrange the entertainment, games, and set up.

"So, all the preparations have been done before some lazy people arrived from Kansas City," Clarence announced with a Cheshire cat grin as Deloris grimaced realizing it was a dig at her. Annoyance written on her face. "How long are you staying, DeDe? Will you be around to help with cleanup?"

"I'm here until Sunday."

"How did you manage to get all that time off?" he asked suspiciously. Deloris knew he was thinking that she must have quit one of her jobs just to come to the picnic. While the picnic was a huge draw and few people missed attending, it wasn't worth losing a job over.

"Well, I have been working extra shifts at Poppy's Paradise Park until they could hire a new soda jerk, so my boss told me he understood my need for some time off and said that I just had to find someone to cover for me. I've got two friends covering that job for me, and at the switchboard, another girl who just started and needs the money is taking my shifts there."

"You want to be careful and not take too much time off. You are lucky to have two jobs and they could fire you at any time."

"Oh, I know. I work extra hard and volunteer to do extra things when they need help, so both of my supervisors like me."

"That's the way to do it." Clarence settled back in his seat, satisfied with Deloris' response.

"Thank you so much for your advice, big brother. I'd be completely, hopelessly lost without you," Deloris replied exaggeratedly, rolling her eyes.

"I know you would be. That's why I get to tell you what to do."

"Sadly, I believe you've been led astray."

"Not at all. It's my constitutional right as your big brother, you know that, right?"

Deloris gave Clarence a friendly punch on the arm before flopping back in her seat in a huff. She considered knocking his hat off, but he was driving, so that probably wasn't a good idea. Instead, she changed the subject. "My turn to ask questions. Did you know Gary Green or his wife or daughter?"

"I knew you were up to something, coming up here on an extended stay. You need to be careful, little Miss Nosey. The murderer is still around, probably."

"I will, Clarence. Just answer my question, please?"

"Yes, I knew Gary Green. He was ten years older than me. We both worked as hired hands on the Worth Farm when I was in high school. He was a no-good, lazy scoundrel when he was younger, and I never saw any improvement as he got older. He was a bully and never could hold a steady job."

"Do you have any idea who could have murdered him?"

"Yeah, the whole town."

"Seriously, Clarence. Do you think his wife or daughter could have murdered him?"

"I think she was his stepdaughter and no. I think it was someone who he cheated out of some money in a poker game or an angry husband who caught him getting fresh with his wife, or just about anyone else whom he may have pushed around and bullied."

"Oh yes, his stepdaughter. I get the feeling that you didn't like him."

"I always steered clear of him as far as I could, which wasn't easy in a small town," Clarence stated flatly.

"I understand that. I just never heard you say anything about this Gary Green. In fact, I never heard of him until I read about him in the newspaper," Deloris added.

"Well, we all breathed a sigh of relief when he disappeared and just thought good riddance. You were only five years old, and you didn't need to know about him. Besides, why talk about someone like that after they're gone? You just move on and hope they don't return."

"What about his wife and stepdaughter?"

"I didn't really know them that well. Thelma knew them better than me. They moved to the farm after Mrs. Green married Gary. She was from Cameron originally. And once Mr. Green disappeared, Mrs. Green mostly stayed on her farm and wasn't in town much. I heard she hired a handyman to help her around the farm."

"I see."

Deloris pulled out her tablet and started making notes of what Clarence had told her. At that moment, the car hit a bump, making her erase and rewrite a word. Then she stuffed it back in her bag as Clarence pulled up to the gate and hopped out of the car to open it. The cows were standing too close to the gate, so he had to slip through it, temporarily latch it and start pushing them away—flailing his arms and hollering to get them to move so he could open the gate wide enough to drive through it. When his mission was accomplished, he pushed the gate open and ran back to the car and put it in gear to drive through. Then he set the brake and hopped out again to close and securely latch the gate. Deloris stayed in the car the entire time.

"Thanks for your help with the gate," Clarence said sarcastically.

"You were having so much fun, I didn't want to interrupt," Deloris replied, batting her eyelashes and giving him her best look of innocence. Clarence tried to glare at her, but had to smile and shake his head. It was hard for him to be angry with her when she gave him that puppy-dog look. Deloris was his baby sister, and he always protected her. He was a little lost when she moved to the city, but now that she was home safely again, he didn't want to sully her visit with a mean word.

About thirty feet in front of the car was the little creek that surrounded the farm. Driving the car over the rock-bottom creek bed, the water barely covered the bottom of the tires. In the spring, the creek was much higher and sometimes Clarence had to leave the car on the gate side of the creek and walk across the tree bridge to get back and forth. But July was typically dry, and the creek was even lower during August. It never dried up completely, thankfully, but it could get down to a trickle.

As they drove up the lane toward the house, Deloris looked around to see if there were any changes to the place, and it comforted her to see only a fresh coat of paint on the house. The horses in the nearby pasture neighed a welcome and the dog, Bonnie, ran toward the car with her tail wagging. Four cats were lounging around on the porch, not caring who came and went.

When Deloris got out of the car, she covered her face with her scarf and held her breath as she quickly walked around the cats into the house before her cat allergies were triggered and she started sneezing. She could smell chicken frying on the cookstove and other aromas of the meal her Momma was fixing. She was home.

CHAPTER 4

Investigation

"Put your things away an' wash up, supper's almost ready," Nannie Markham told her daughter when she entered the kitchen.

"Hello to you too, mother," Deloris replied.

"Oh yes, sorry. Hello Deloris. I'm just concentrating on trying to get everything ready for tomorrow."

The old cook stove was heating up the house with potatoes boiling in one pot and corn on the cob boiling in another. On the front burner was Nannie's large cast-iron skillet filled with sizzling golden-brown chicken. Nannie stood over the chicken, turning the pieces while the grease popped and splatted on her full apron.

"Momma, can I help you?"

"Yes dear, set the table an' slice up some tomatoes and cucumbers, then put the radishes an' green onions on the table."

Deloris did as she was told. As she cleaned the vegetables at the sink, she noticed six pies cooling in the windowsill: two rhubarb, two gooseberry, and two apple. Deloris knew that most of the pies were for the picnic, because every year the call went out to the local women to bake pies and donate them to the cookshack so that they could be sold by the slice to attendees. Then there was the baking competition where Momma usually entered her pies and light rolls. Thelma's light rolls won a couple of times before she moved to Kansas City, beating even her Momma's rolls. Nannie had been so proud of her daughter for that accomplishment.

"Momma," Deloris said after a few minutes.

"Yes?"

"Who do you think killed Gary Green?"

"Deloris!" Nannie chastised. "We ain't gonna talk about that now."

"But Momma, I never heard you talk about him, or Mrs. Green, or her daughter.

"Yes, and there's a reason. It ain't none of our business what goes on in their family. Good folk don't gossip about their neighbors. Now get along now and finish up. The chicken's almost done."

"But Momma, if Mrs. Green or her daughter are innocent, we can't just stand by and see them go to jail for something they didn't do."

With her tongs poised above the skillet, Nannie gave an exasperated sigh and turned to face her daughter. With a look of consternation upon her face, she said, "Well, ain't that the sheriff's job? They don't know where the daughter is, anyway. They can't find her, an' Mrs. Green is now Mrs. Gibbs, so she has a husband to stand by her."

"What?"

"Yes, Sarah Green married her hired hand, Oliver Gibbs, 'bout five days ago. They went to Gallatin an' got a Justice of the Peace. Seems now she knows Gary Green is dead; she can finally go on with her life. Stands to reason that she don't think she's goin' to jail iffen she just got married."

Deloris wished she had brought her tablet downstairs with her, so she made a mental note to write it down later when she went up to her room.

When supper was on the table, Nannie went outside to holler at the menfolk to come inside. Sometimes she rang the large cast iron dinner bell that stood on a post near the door, but they were only in the barn milking and not in the field, so they could hear her call. Within minutes, all the men came to the house and washed up before sitting down at the table.

Besides Will, Deloris' father, and her brother Clarence, Deloris' parents had one hired hand, Clifford Candy, who ate supper with them.

Clifford was a neighbor boy that Nannie took care of after his mother died when he was twelve years old. His father died five years before that, and Clifford had no other family. He was overly shy and seldom talked to people, especially girls. When Clifford was ten years old, he quietly walked out of school in the fourth grade, vowing to his mother that he would never return, and he never did.

After Clifford's parents died, Nannie felt sorry for him and invited him to come live with the Markhams, but Clifford turned her down, instead accepting a job as their hired hand. He mostly lived in one of three caves on his parents' farm, and only went into the house there when Nannie came to bring him food or to check on him when he was sick. Clifford was smart, fantastic with numbers, and could figure up how many bushels of corn to the acre they could expect, all in his head. He just didn't like people very much, even though he also worked for other folks as a hired hand when needed. Deloris wanted to find out if he'd ever worked on the Green's farm. He might know something, but unless someone asked him directly what he knew, Clifford wouldn't say anything. Her father helped her out, though, bringing up Gary's name and mentioning the murder, much to Nannie's dismay. It turned out that Clifford had worked shucking corn for Gary Green once, but didn't like him. "He hit me," Clifford said, rubbing his cheek. But before Deloris could ask a question, Nannie shut the conversation down before it went any further.

When supper was finished, Deloris helped Nannie with the dishes while the men sat out on the back porch talking. She wanted to figure out how to ask Clifford a few questions about Gary Green, but knew that she'd have to go about it carefully. Clifford didn't talk to girls, except Nannie. Even though he and Deloris played together when they were younger, he quit talking to her once she grew up. He now shied away from her like he did with all the other girls.

When the dishes were done, she went out on the back porch and sat down next to Clifford, who immediately moved to the other side of the porch.

"Clifford, don't you remember me?" Deloris pleaded. "We used to play together on this very porch."

Will and Clarence watched on as she tried to lure Clifford into trusting her.

"I...I know Miss DeDe, but you growed up. I liked you when you was young," he said nervously.

"Oh Clifford, I'm the same person. Here I brought you something from the city."

Deloris held out a small wooden game to Clifford that she picked up at the train station where one peg is jumped over another like in checkers until only one peg remains.

Clifford didn't turn to her, but looked at the game with one eye.

"Go on, take it," Deloris encouraged. "I bought it just for you. It's yours."

Clifford turned toward Deloris, looking at the game in her hand. Then he reached out. She handed it to him and he immediately turned away again, looking at his new prize.

Deloris turned toward her father and brought up the subject of the murder, hoping Clifford would chime in with any information he might know.

"Deloris, your mother doesn't like to discuss the subject," her father chided, since he was just reprimanded for doing it, too.

"I know, but I am fascinated with the story and I want to know more." Deloris looked pleadingly at her father.

Will leaned forward and looked through the backdoor into the kitchen where Nannie was wrapping up the pies for the picnic in tea towels.

"I guess it wouldn't hurt to discuss it a little," he said quietly. Deloris knew she was the apple of her father's eye, and he found it very hard to say no to his little girl.

"Good," Deloris said as she pulled out her pencil and tablet, then leaned in to hear better. She whispered, "What can you tell me about Gary Green?"

"Well, I knew his parents better than him," Will said. "His parents were good people, but they let Gary control them and his little sister. If Gary didn't like it, they didn't do it. His sister got married at fifteen and immediately moved away. Her parents gave her the bed she was sleeping on as a wedding present, and that was the extent of her inheritance. When his parents died, Gary took over the farm and sold everything that was loose and not vital to running the farm. This included some of the farm equipment and animals.

Gary squandered all the money he got from selling these things on drinking, gambling, and, well, uh. He almost lost the farm a time or two, but an uncle bailed him out because he felt sorry for Mrs. Green."

"What Dad is trying to say is that he went to Kansas City and spent a lot of his money on women of the night," Clarence inserted.

Will turned a bright shade of red and scolded, "Clarence!"

"Well, it is true, isn't it?"

"Oh, I see," Deloris said thoughtfully.

Deloris then turned to Clifford and asked him, "Clifford, I understand you knew Gary Green."

Clifford had been listening to Will and Clarence, but suddenly leaned back, away from the conversation.

"Clifford, you knew him, didn't you? You worked with him shucking corn, didn't you?" she pressed.

"Yes, but he was a very mean man. He hit me a lot."

Looking surprised, Clarence turned to Clifford and said, "He hit you a lot?"

"Yes." Clifford rubbed his jaw in remembrance.

"I didn't know that, or I would have taken care of him for you and made him leave you alone."

"It's okay, Mr. Clarence. I took care of him."

Everyone on the back porch had a startled look upon their faces at this revelation.

"Clifford, how did you take care of Gary Green?" Deloris persisted.

"I don't want to say!" and at that Clifford jumped up and ran into the house.

"Y-y-you don't think..." Deloris stammered.

"No, no. Clifford wouldn't hurt a fly. He probably just

took something of Gary's and hid it," Will said with a worried look on his face.

Deloris could see that the discussion was over for the time being and went into the house to talk to her mother.

"What did you say to Clifford? He went running through here and out the front door like the house was on fire!"

"I just asked him a question."

"Mm-hmm." Exasperated at Deloris' persistence, Nannie drew in a deep breath and continued, "I heare'd what y'all were talkin' 'bout and I don't want ta hear another word about the Greens. We need to be focusin' upon the picnic."

"Okay, Momma."

CHAPTER 5

The Picnic

Thursday morning, Nannie and Clarence left early for the picnic grounds to turn in her donation of two pies, a peck of vine-ripened tomatoes, and half a peck of onions. Nannie stayed at the cookshack to help clean up the kitchen and knock the cobwebs off of things, while Clarence helped set up the games and got the chairs and horseshoes out of storage. Will and Clifford had some fence mending on the farm to do, so they stayed behind, as did Deloris, who was left at home to sleep in.

At ten, Nannie and Clarence returned so that Nannie could get lunch ready. Sitting around the table, everyone discussed the picnic and who Nannie and Clarence had seen earlier. Deloris asked what time everyone was going back up to the fairgrounds, and Nannie said that she and Will would go up that evening. "I need to get my baking and chores done 'afore we head back to town," she explained.

Deloris then turned to her big brother, Clarence, and asked, "When are you going to the picnic?"

"I wasn't going to go at all today," he replied, trying to look innocent.

Folding her hands under her chin and looking at her brother with big eyes, Deloris pleaded, "Will you take me to the picnic grounds today, pleeeaaassse?"

Clarence snickered. "Oh all right. I'll take you up right after lunch. I still have some work to do there, anyway."

At this revelation, Deloris glared at him. "You *were* going up anyway, weren't you?"

"Maybe," he replied with a wry grin.

"Oh, you!" Deloris blurted out in frustration.

"Are you going to try your luck in the Talent Show?" Clarence asked her with a wink. He obviously had talked with Bert and knew about the smart-alecky comment about the talent show in the letter she sent Deloris, because he knew Deloris couldn't sing on key. She could dance, but Momma didn't allow her to do that.

Deloris was sitting in Clarence's car ready to go. As soon as he finished his work and cleaned up, he hopped in his car and looked over at her.

"Have you been sitting in the car all this time? Why?"

"I didn't want you to accidentally forget me. I know how you can get busy and forget things at your age."

Grumbling to himself, Clarence put the car in gear and the siblings were off for the picnic. He angle parked on the east side of the park near the tractor pull site. Deloris bounded out of the car and walked over to the bandstand on the north side of the park, while Clarence went to where the horseshoe games were being set up.

No one was near the bandstand since the picnic didn't officially start for another few hours and most folks were busy working in the cookshack or setting up the games. Deloris casually walked behind the bandstand, mostly out of sight from the rest of the picnic grounds, and bent down to look underneath. The boards around the bottom of the bandstand were in a latticework design, painted white with a nearby sign advising, *Don't touch wet paint*. Next to the stairs, she found a little door built into the tightly lattice-worked wall that opened easily, so she slipped inside. It was dark and foreboding under there. Mainly, she wanted to see where the body was found. She saw where the original posts stood, and where the ground had been dug up near the right side, midway between where two pillars would have supported the bandstand when it was smaller. That made sense, she thought. If Green's body had been in the middle or towards the back, someone might have seen the freshly dug earth through the lattice door when it was open. But it was hard to see through the tightly woven lattice work on the sides, making the rest of the space invisible. There weren't many people who would have been up around the bandstand to see it, anyway. While it was the city park, the playground equipment was on the south side, and that's where people usually gathered, unless the bandstand was in use for the picnic or Fourth of July. And if he was buried there sometime after the picnic, then no one would have been around the bandstand for several months.

The floor of the original bandstand was raised about five feet, so a taller person would need to bend over to dig the hole. While this bandstand was wider, it seemed the same height as the old one. Deloris pulled out her tablet and walked over toward the open door to get enough light to see to write her observation. At five-foot-two, she could have almost walked straight in. When she finished looking around and writing, she bent down slightly under the opening and walked out. As she closed the lattice door, she got white paint on her right hand. Great, she thought, how will I explain this to Momma?

She carefully brushed the dirt off her dress and shoes with her left hand, then walked over to the cookshack to try to wash the white paint off of her hand and see who might be working. The cookshack kitchen had a row of screened windows on two sides for ventilation. The north side was a solid wall and the south side had the serving counter, which was a partial wall with a screen on the top and short curtains to serve food through on a counter. On the serving side, people could walk up to a row of tables dividing them from the workers and place their orders. Behind the customers was a condiment table that would later be filled with tomatoes, onions, pickles, mustard, and ketchup. There were three long rows of narrow picnic tables with benches where customers could sit to eat. Above the serving window was a blackboard that listed the various pies. On the servers' right was the screened-in pie safe. The cream pies were kept inside the kitchen in an icebox. On the servers' left was a cooler filled with soda pop and ice water.

Deloris opened the door on the back side of the cookshack and walked inside. She found Nellie Robertson and Maude Fine happily working away, forming hamburger patties and putting them in layers on a large sheet. In between each layer, they used a new invention—wax paper—that worked wonderfully to prevent the hamburgers from sticking to each other. Another woman, Mrs. Moira Harvey, the banker's wife, was setting out packages of hamburger buns and cutting cheese to put on the burgers. Mrs. Bessie Simpson, from Simpson's Hardware Store, was dipping pork tenderloins in egg and rolling them in bread crumbs before putting them on a sheet and covering them in wax paper.

PECULIARITIES AT THE PICNIC

Noticing Deloris, Maude nodded in recognition and asked, "Deloris, hello. How are you? Up for the picnic, I see."

"Hello Mrs. Fine." Deloris smiled. "Yes, you know I can't miss the picnic. Do you mind if I wash my hands in here?"

"Sure, go ahead. You can use the dipper over there and put some water in the wash pan." Maude noticed with surprise that Deloris had paint on her hands.

"I see you got into the paint?"

"Oh, yes, I can't be within five feet of fresh paint without getting some on me," Deloris said, laughing. "I wanted to see the new bandstand; Clarence was telling me all about how Old Man Jones rebuilt it so quickly after the tornado."

Then Deloris looked over at Lara Cogswell, who was slicing onions and had tears running down her face. With a concerned look, Deloris asked, "Are you all right?"

"Oh, yes, dear. I'm just slicing onions," Lara replied with a smile through her tears.

"Oh, silly me. I thought you might be crying over the skeleton they found under the bandstand."

Everything went silent among the women, then Maude Fine said, "This is picnic time. We aren't discussing any of that here."

Deloris realized they were closing ranks and not going to offer her any additional information; coming to the cookshack had backfired. She said a polite goodbye and left. Outside the cookshack, she looked around the park once more and saw everyone else hard at work. Instead of interrupting them, she decided to take a stroll down Main Street to see what stores might be open and talk to some merchants, at least the ones she thought might be more open to discussing the murder.

CHAPTER 6
Main Street

Standing at the north end of Main Street, Deloris looked down at the bustling business district of Jameson, Missouri, and tried to etch it into her mind. She knew not much had changed since it first transitioned from Feurt Summit to Jameson in 1871.

To Deloris' left was the printing office where Mr. Peterson printed *The Jameson Gem* every week. She could hear the printing press going in the back of the shop and decided not to go inside, while he was busy trying to get the newspaper finished. She studied the street, trying to plan out which merchants would talk to her and which ones wouldn't.

Next to the newspaper office was the butcher's shop. The butcher was constantly busy with customers, so she skipped his shop. He scared her anyway. When she was a young girl, she entered his shop and saw him cutting up a customer's order. He had blood on his hands and apron. Then when he used his sleeve to wipe his brow it left a smear of blood on his face too. Deloris stood there petrified unable to speak, until he barked, "Well, what do you want?"

Just past his shop was the First National Bank. She wanted to talk with someone on a more personal basis, so the bank, where several people were sure to be inside and listening curiously to her conversation, was out, too.

Mrs. Moira Harvey's Tea and Coffee Shop shared the bank building. Mrs. Harvey was a transplant from England who attempted to turn Jameson into a quaint English village with her fancy tablecloths, silver sets, China dishes, and specially brewed tea. Her shop was only open for teatime from two until five o'clock. Deloris was in there once, when her home economics class was taught how to set a proper table and other table manners. Since Mrs. Harvey was up at the cookshack, she knew her shop would be closed. "I'll just come back to her later when I can talk with her in private," Deloris thought to herself.

Above the bank building and Harvey's Tea and Coffee Shop was the Opera House and Theater, where Deloris and her friends often spent Friday nights, swooning over Rudoph Valentino, Ronald Colman or Douglas Fairbanks, or rooting for Mary Pickford and Mae West. Deloris first became enthralled in the moving pictures when her aunt took her as a youngster to see *The Perils of Pauline*.

After the Theater was Robertson's Mercantile & Millinery Store. It was obviously closed, since Nellie Robertson was at the cookshack too.

The barbershop next door had four or five customers sitting around talking. When Deloris appeared at the window, everyone stopped talking and watched her. She paused, nodded a greeting, and then continued walking down the street. Though she would have loved to talk to everyone inside, for her to enter the barbershop would have caused quite the stir—a female in a male-only establishment. Momma would have had words to say about that!

PECULIARITIES AT THE PICNIC

Next was Thompson's General Store. It was open, and going inside, Deloris found Alphia Thompson sweeping the floor. Alphia's father was in the back, checking the latest deliveries. Alphia, called Alfie by her friends and family, was Deloris' classmate until they both graduated from Jameson High School and was one of her best friends in Jameson.

"Hey Alfie! How are you?"

"DeDe, when did you get into town?" Alfie asked as she stopped sweeping and leaned the broom up against a shelf to give Deloris a hug.

"I came up on the train yesterday afternoon."

"I'm sure glad to see you! Did you hear about the bones they found?" she asked conspiratorially.

At last, Deloris had found a kindred spirit. "Yes, I read it in the newspaper. What are people saying about who did it?"

"They don't know, and no one is really talking. Of course, the sheriff suspects Mrs. Green or her new husband, but people say it was this man from Bethany that threatened Mr. Green, saying he owed him money for a car he sold him."

"Really? Do you know the man's name?"

"Nelson or Needham or Narry something. Sorry, I just don't remember."

"Interesting," Deloris said as she pulled out her tablet and wrote this down. "Bethany, you said?"

"Yes, I'm pretty sure of that. Are you investigating the murder like you did the one in Poppy's Paradise Park that you wrote about in your last letter? Did you find the murderer?"

"Hold on. One question at a time. Yes, I found the murderer, but I'll tell you about it later. Right now, I have a short amount of time to focus on this mystery. I am curious, especially with it happening right here in Jameson" Deloris admitted. "But don't tell anyone, please. Momma would be upset if she found out I was asking questions about it. Do you think Mrs. Green, sorry, Mrs. Gibbs, or her daughter, Lucinda, had anything to do with it?"

"I don't..." Alfie began, but before she could finish her sentence, Mrs. Gibbs herself walked into the store.

Alfie's eyes got as big as saucers and she stood there, frozen for a minute. Mrs. Gibbs didn't say a word, but looked at both girls before lowering her head, knowing that they must have been talking about her. Deloris saw this as her chance to talk with her.

"Hello Mrs. Green, I mean, I heard it is Mrs. Gibbs now. I am so happy for you," Deloris said with her cheeriest smile.

"Thank you," Sarah said in a soft, dulcet tone.

Deloris persisted, "I just want to say that I am so sorry for your loss and for all the rumors flying around. I want to help you."

Sarah looked up into Deloris' eyes to see if she was sincere and, seeing that she was, wondered why. Then she said, "How can you help? I don't think anyone can help me."

Deloris hid her hand in the folds of her skirt and crossed her fingers as she said, "I work at the Kansas City Police Department and I have solved a murder or two there. I believe you are innocent and I want to try to prove it, if you will allow me."

Okay, that wasn't exactly true about what her job was at the Kansas City Police Department, but at least she did work there, and Deloris needed to convince Mrs. Gibbs that she was serious.

"Well, if you really think that, you can help," Sarah said slowly.

"I do. May I visit with you at your home and ask you a few questions? I am only up here for the picnic and will leave Sunday to go back to Kansas City. May I come tomorrow morning or early afternoon?"

"I guess it can't hurt. Tomorrow morning around 9 a.m. will be best for me."

"I'll be there," Deloris said triumphantly.

Sarah Gibbs hurried through the store gathering her groceries and then walked to the counter in the back where Alfie's father had just arrived from the backroom.

Deloris was so excited to have the opportunity to talk with Mrs. Green—Gibbs—that she could barely hide her smile. She gave Alfie a wink as she turned to walk out of the store, but before she did, she turned back to her friend. Alfie had witnessed the entire exchange, and she appeared mesmerized at Deloris' courage.

Deloris asked Alfie, "Will I see you at the picnic tonight?"

"Oh yes, I'll be there."

Back out on Main Street, Deloris saw Nellie Robertson returning to her store, so Deloris retraced her steps. When she got to Robertson's Mercantile and Millinery, Nellie was just unlocking the front door. As Mrs. Robertson turned the sign that hung on the door to Open, she glanced up at Deloris and then quickly turned the sign back to Closed. Re-locking the door from the inside, she disappeared into the back of the store. That was rather curious, Deloris thought as she stood there for a moment staring in disbelief at the sign. With a shrug, she continued back down the street to the Jameson Farmer's Bank.

Peering inside, she saw a former classmate, Dorothy

Smith, counting money in the teller's cage. Mr. Harvey, the bank president, was sitting in his office to the left of the teller cages talking to Craig Ness, a local farmer. Everyone looked busy, so Deloris decided not to enter the bank and ask questions.

She turned the corner at 2nd Street and there it was, her most favorite place in all of Jameson—Ma Robbins' Restaurant. It was funny how things were bigger in your memories than they actually are, Deloris thought. Robbins' Restaurant looked so small now compared to when Deloris and her friends hung out there after school. As she pushed open the door, a bell rang, announcing her entrance. Mrs. Robbins, whom everyone called Ma Robbins, emerged from the little kitchen in back to stand behind the three-stool counter. Ma Robbins had the neatest things in her restaurant, including a wind-up Victor Phonograph Gramophone in the corner with and a cooler filled with soda pop in ice water beside it. In the other corner, near the door that Deloris had just entered, was a shuffleboard table. How she fit everything into this tiny space was a miracle.

"Why, Deloris! How are you, dear? How is your mom?" Ma Robbins asked warmly.

"I'm fine, and my Momma is fine, too," Deloris answered with a smile.

"Let's see. You graduated this year, didn't you?"

"Yes, I graduated in May and went to Kansas City to live with my sister, Thelma."

"Well, isn't that something? You're up for the picnic, I suppose?"

"Yes, you know I can't miss the picnic. It would almost seem sinful to miss it." Deloris laughed, as did Ma.

"What can I get for you, hon?"

Deloris wasn't really hungry, since she'd just eaten

lunch, but she wanted a reason to stay and talk to Ma Robbins, so she asked, "May I have a burger, French fries and a Coke?"

"Sure thing. Let's see, do you still want your burger medium rare?"

"You remembered!"

"Well, it hasn't been that long ago when you were sitting on that very stool with your friends ordering the same thing."

"That is true," Deloris smiled at the memory.

"You aren't going to wait and eat at the cookshack tonight?"

"I figure I can eat there tomorrow night, but I wanted to get one of your cheeseburgers while I am in town, too."

At that, Ma Robbins smiled and nodded in approval. Then she went into the back room to where she prepared the food. From there, she yelled out, "So, how is life in the big city?"

"It's good. I work two jobs, you know." Deloris raised her voice to be heard.

"No, I didn't know. Where do you work?"

"I work at the Kansas City Police Department through the week and at the soda fountain at Poppy's Paradise Park on weekends. Austin Martin works at the police department, too. He helped me get the job there."

"Well, isn't that something?"

When Ma Robbins brought Deloris her food, Deloris figured it was a good time to start a conversation about the murder.

"May I ask you a question?"

"Certainly, hon," Ma Robbins said as she perched on a stool behind the counter.

"Do you think Mrs. Green, I mean Mrs. Gibbs, or her daughter, killed Gary Green?"

A quick look of surprise crossed Ma Robbins' face before she answered.

"Not for a minute do I believe they killed that good-for-nothing rapist and two-bit gambler, nor do I think Lucinda's boyfriend did it either."

"Lucinda's boyfriend?"

"Oh, I've heard some folks speculate that he may have killed Gary Green, but we'll never know."

"Why is that?"

"Because he was killed in the Great War."

"What was his name?"

"Amos Conaway. But listen, sweetheart, you'd be wise not to pursue who did kill Gary Green. It isn't really important now." Ma Robbins crossed her arms and shivered. "Everyone in town disliked him and they were all much happier with him gone. He owed almost everyone in town, and I heard he raped several women. Gary bullied people, extorting money out of them, and he was just an all-around mean-hearted person. I suspect several people wanted to murder him at various times, but I don't think Sarah or Lucinda had the gumption to do it. He tried to get friendly with me, but my hubby scared him off with a shotgun."

"I had no idea," said Deloris, shocked by all of this.

Ma Robbins nodded, and continued, "Boney Garrison accused him of stealing some money out of his house and, the next thing you know, his car burned up right out in front of his house. A guy in Bethany came to town saying that Gary owed him money. Sean O'Casey had him arrested for stealing some of his cows and then Sean's barn mysteriously burned down. He hired Emmett to help him rebuild it. Speaking of Sean, he appears to be in a might better mood lately. Can't figure that guy out. He goes around for years grumbling. He was always complaining about this thing or that, and now he's all helpful and speaking kindly. Go figure."

"I see," Deloris said thoughtfully as she pulled out her tablet and wrote something down.

"What have you got there?" Ma asked.

"Oh, it's just my Big Chief tablet where I'm writing my observations and what people say. I apparently didn't pack my notebook that I usually take with me when I talk to people so I grabbed this."

"You aren't going to tell anyone what I said, are you?"

"Oh no, I'm not putting down your name," Deloris reassured her. "This is just for me to read. You know I like a good mystery, and this one is right in my hometown!"

Ma Robbins shook her head. "Deloris, you need to be careful. This isn't a game." Laying a hand on Deloris' arm, she continued, "Somebody murdered Gary Green. You go digging around, bringing up old problems, and somebody might get desperate. Desperate people do desperate things, and you don't want to get hurt if they think that you're getting close."

Deloris sat up straighter. "I'll be careful. I do have some experience helping Austin Martin—and solving murders," Deloris said proudly. Okay, it may have only been one murder, but no one up home really knew that she was exaggerating, she thought to herself. Except for Austin himself, but she didn't think he'd rat her out, he'd just give her a lecture.

After finishing her cheeseburger, Deloris said goodbye to Ma and stepped outside. South of Ma Robbins' Restaurant was the garage. The garage door was open, but when she peeked inside, she didn't see anyone. There was a sign saying "Back Soon," so the mechanic must have gone to run an errand. That was unfortunate, Deloris thought, because the garage was another local gossip station for all the men in town, especially Old Man Jones. Everyone in town knew about the gossip circle in the garage where several men could be seen sitting around smoking, drinking, and telling tall tales of legendary proportions. Maybe all the men must have been up at the picnic helping set up. It could help in her investigation to hear a few of those tall tales right now, but she decided to return later.

Next to the garage was Bowman's Hardware Store. A portion of the store was used for the post office, with Mr. Bowman serving as the town's postmaster alongside owning his business. Deloris poked her head in to find Mr. Bowman sorting mail and getting ready to make his deliveries. He looked busy, so she decided to talk to him later. That only left the small café on this side of the street, and Deloris was so full right now she couldn't imagine ordering anything else. It was time to go back to the picnic grounds anyway, before Clarence realized she'd disappeared. She'd come back later to try her luck at the rest of the businesses.

CHAPTER 7
Back to the Picnic

More people were starting to show up when Deloris arrived back at the picnic grounds. The mayor was doing a microphone check up on the bandstand stage and talking with two other men who were standing on the ground below, ready to assist him.

She walked over to the east side of the bandstand where a few men were starting a game of horseshoes. Moving closer, she noticed that the two men in charge of the horseshoe games were using a type of abacus to keep track of each player's wins. She could hear one of them claim that this was actually the practice round.

Behind them was the space provided for the tractor- and horse-pulling contest. The dirt had been leveled and two skids, each loaded with one ton of rocks, waited for the first contestants to see how much more weight needed to be added based upon the weight and horsepower of the tractor.

She saw Mr. Peterson, the editor of *The Jameson Gem*, also walking around, talking to the various folks about the preparations and jotting down a few notes. He must have finished printing the newspaper he was working earlier.

Deloris sidled up to him and asked, "Hello, Mr. Peterson. Have you learned any more about the murder investigation here?"

"No, I haven't heard any more than what I printed in the paper a few weeks ago. But if I find out anything more, you can be sure it'll be in the paper," he responded brusquely.

Feeling dismissed, she thanked him and then walked back to the main park grounds and to the cookshack. As she approached it, she overheard her name mentioned inside the kitchen. When the women working there saw Deloris at the door, they stopped what they were doing to look at her. The awkward silence told Deloris that her presence wasn't welcome in their circle of friends. Feeling like an outsider in her own hometown, Deloris turned and stiffly walked away, feeling the eyes of everyone in the cookshack.

Just then, Old Man Jones' pickup pulled up behind the cookshack, with the back filled to the top with a load of watermelons. Bart Shaw and Corny Higgins hopped out and started unloading the juicy, delicious fruits, putting them in a water tank that was filled with blocks of ice and water. When they finished, Mr. Robertson dropped in another two blocks of ice and the boys started chipping away at them with an ice pick. Old Man Jones then parked the truck on the other side of the bandstand.

As he climbed out, Deloris went over to him and said, "Excuse me, Mr. Jones, may I ask you a few questions?

"Sure can, little lady. Whatcha need?"

"I'm Will Markham's daughter and..."

"Yar. I hain't seen you since you were knee high to a grasshopper. How is old Will doin?"

"He's doing fine. He'll be here soon. I was wondering about the bones that you found under the bandstand."

PECULIARITIES AT THE PICNIC

"Now, why would you worry your pretty little head about something as bad as that?"

"I'm trying to help Mrs. Green, I mean Gibbs. I understand the sheriff thinks she is guilty of murdering her husband. That's what it said in *The Jameson Gem*. Do you think she did it? Or did Lucinda? Or even Amos Conaway?"

"Oh horsefeathers! No, I don't think she or her little girl or Amos did it. Amos was a hero. Got a plaque dedicated to him on the courthouse lawn, the post office wall and everywhere else. Why, I had half a mind to kill Gary Green myself, a time or two."

"Do you have any idea who may have killed him, so that I can help Mrs. Gibbs?"

"Nah, there was a fella through here a long time ago looking for him. Said he sold Gary a car and Gary never paid him. He may have found him, or maybe a jealous husband caught up with him."

"Did you get the man's name or any information about him?"

"Can't say that I did, and it was a long time ago, so even iffa I heared it, I don't remember it now."

"Is there anything else you can remember about the time Gary Green went missing?"

Old Man Jones shook his head no, saying, "People say that he burnt down Sean O'Casey's barn and I woulda been madder than a wet hen if he burnt my barn down. I helped Sean rebuild it. Yeah, me and Sean O'Casey ran him offa our property more than once. He was a no good, yella-bellied, egg-sucking dog. I tell ya."

"You and Sean O'Casey?"

"Well, Gary was snooping around and neither one of us trusted him no further than we could of throwed him."

"Okay, thank you, Mr. Jones."

"Quite all right, little lady. But like I said, don't you worry your head none at all. Sheriff'll figure it out. Tell your pa to come see me."

"I will," Deloris replied. After a pause, she added, "But could you tell me anything else about Mr. Green?"

"Nah," he replied, and then to Deloris' disappointment he changed the subject, asking, "Now, did I ever tell you about the time your pa, Clarence, and I went to the auction in Chillicothe? Well—"

"I'm sorry," Deloris interrupted, knowing that once Old Man Jones got started telling stories she'd never get away "but maybe you could tell me later? I need to find Clarence. Thank you so much for your help! Goodbye!"

Old Man Jones looked a little surprised at her rudeness, cutting him off from telling his story, but he tipped his hat and said goodbye as she waved and hurried off.

Deloris wandered around the park and finally found Clarence on the other side of the tree line to the north of the park. This was Sean O'Casey's property, where targets had been set up for the rifle sharpshooting contest. His property was on both sides of the road north of the picnic grounds. Deloris' father was an excellent marksman with a rifle or a pistol and was the reigning champion in the county, having won the last four years running. In his youth he'd even beat Wyatt Earp in a sharpshooting contest out in Kansas, or so Deloris had heard. Last year at the picnic, Clarence came in second place and Deloris guessed he planned to give his father a run for his money this year.

As soon as the men looked like they were done setting up the targets, Deloris walked up to Clarence and asked him if he could take her home.

PECULIARITIES AT THE PICNIC

"What's the matter, DeDe? The picnic is just getting started."

"Well, it's funny, but after only being gone three months, suddenly I feel like an outsider trying to get at the truth. I believe people know what happened to Gary Green, but either they don't care, or they want to protect the murderer. Even Old Man Jones only told me a little, and he's usually an encyclopedia."

"You must know that this wouldn't end well. Jameson is a close-knit community and when one in the flock is hurting, they close ranks to protect them. They're not against you, they just don't want to dredge up old gossip that might hurt someone innocent."

"I know, but I thought I was one of the flock."

"Well, maybe if you stick around longer, you'll hear more. There'll be folks at the picnic tonight from out of town, maybe even from Cameron, where Mrs. Green was from, who might talk to you."

"Okay," Deloris relented.

Clarence gave her a hug and then said with a devilish smile, "Besides, I don't really want to lose my parking spot."

Deloris almost stuck her tongue out at him, but she stopped herself when she remembered she needed a favor. "I need to ask you something else. Will you take me to Sarah Gibbs' house tomorrow at nine o'clock?"

"What have you done now?"

"I saw her at Thompsons' General Store and she agreed to let me talk with her."

"Deloris ..."

"Please."

"Oh, all right," Clarence said resignedly. "Now go enjoy the picnic, DeDe."

CHAPTER 8

Back to Main Street

Deloris left Clarence, but instead of going back to the park, she decided to walk back to Main Street, hoping she could catch a few more people before everything closed up for the picnic. She just couldn't believe that no one would say anything about the murder of Gary Green. Jameson was a small town; folks knew their neighbors there. Someone would know something.

As she walked down the street, she found the printing office and the banks closed. Mrs. Harvey's shop appeared to still be closed, but the garage was open and Mush Evans, the owner, was there. She peeked inside and then entered the inner sanctum of the men's hangout. There she found Mush with his back to her, fixing the inner tube on a tire.

"Hello, Mr. Evans."

Slightly jumping, he said, "Oh, hello. You gave me a fright."

"I'm sorry. I didn't mean to startle you. Someone had a flat tire, huh?" Deloris asked smoothly.

"Yeah, Tom Fine needs it fixed today."

"I bet he does. May I bother you to ask a question or two?"

"Sure, whatcha got?" He turned toward her, wiping his hands on a rag.

Deloris got straight to the point. "What do you think about Gary Green's murder? Do you know where his daughter is?"

"Well, that ain't a question about transmissions, is it?" Mush thought for a moment and said, "I don't know very much. I only moved to Jameson and opened up this shop eleven years ago and didn't know Gary Green. That also means that I never knew his daughter either. That was a long time ago and even if I did know, I wouldn't say." He shrugged. "From what I've heard, the town is better off with him gone. Sorry, I can't help you."

"Okay, thank you, anyway," Deloris said. "I'll come back when I have a question about transmissions." Mush laughed, and she said goodbye.

Continuing on down the street, she found Mr. Bowman in his hardware store, writing in his receipt book.

"Hello."

"Oh hello," Mr. Bowman looked up. "What can I do for you?"

"I was wondering if you have any idea who may have killed Gary Green?" Deloris asked boldly.

"Well, that's pretty straightforward," he replied, affronted by her brazen attitude. "No, I don't, but if I did, I still wouldn't say. He stole some things from my store and when I confronted him, he laughed and told me I couldn't prove it. I hated him. I don't know who killed him, and I don't care."

"What about Lucinda Hawkins? Have you seen any mail from her?"

PECULIARITIES AT THE PICNIC

"No, can't say that I have and couldn't tell you if I did," he replied firmly.

"Okay, thank you, Mr. Bowman." Deloris left, a little crestfallen that she didn't get more information from her hometown people.

A little café sat on the southeast side of Main Street. Inside she found Mr. Whitestone sitting behind the empty counter with a small black fan busily stirring up the warm air. At the tinkle of the bell over the door, he stood up and said, "Howdy. What can I get you?"

"Oh, uh, how about a grape soda?" Deloris asked. She was already stuffed from eating Momma's big lunch, and then the cheeseburger, but she needed to order something or she'd have no reason to be in the cafe.

"Sure enough."

He walked around the counter to the huge cooler that had all flavors of soda pop with the top of their bottles sticking out of icy cold water. He pulled out the grape Polly's Pop, placed the bottle in the opener, and pulled up. The cap popped off and landed with a collection of other caps below the opener. He then set the pop on the counter in front of her. She watched a small piece of ice following a path down the side of the bottle as she reached into her purse. She handed Mr. Whitestone a nickel, took a drink, and set the bottle back in the water ring it left on the counter.

"Hey, aren't you Will Markham's girl?" Mr. Whitestone asked.

"Yes, sir. I am."

"How's he doing? I haven't seen him in a while."

"Oh, you know. He's busy either fixing fence, tending to the farm animals or harvesting a crop. There's always something to be done on a farm."

"I know that is true," he said with a nod.

"Mr. Whitestone," Deloris began, "I was wondering if you have any thoughts about Gary Green's murder that took place here fourteen years ago. Who do you think might have done it?"

"Oh, I have thoughts on it all right, but all I'm going to say is that I am surprised it didn't happen sooner. Drinking, gambling, robbing, and cheating can get a person dead," as he said this, he knocked his knuckles on the counter for emphasis that he wasn't going to say any more.

"So, he wasn't a very nice man, I take it."

"No, he wasn't a very nice man." At that, Mr. Whitestone suddenly turned away from Deloris and started rearranging some things on the back shelf behind the counter. Then he left out the back, taking some boxes to the burn pile. He seemed to be purposefully staying busy to avoid any more conversation with her.

Deloris stayed put, determined to learn more. After about fifteen minutes later, he finally returned.

"Oh, you're still here," he said, surprised, and Deloris nodded, hoping he'd say something else, but he didn't, so she finished her drink in silence.

When she turned to leave, Mr. Whitestone said, "Tell your pa I said hello and to come see me when he can."

"I will."

Mr. Whitestone's cafe was shaded and cool, so as Deloris stepped out into the blazing hot sun, she pulled her hat down to shield her eyes, squinting until they became accustomed to the bright sunlight. Crossing to the west side of Main Street, she headed back toward the picnic grounds. She walked past Doc Graham's office with its "Closed" sign on the door and continued northward.

The lumberyard sat at the back of the lot between Doc

Graham's office and a brand-new telephone building. She skipped the lumberyard because she couldn't think of a good excuse to go in. Anyway, she really wanted to talk with Mrs. Frankie Martin, Jameson's telephone operator, so she walked there instead. Who better would know what was going on in Jameson than Mrs. Martin? Besides, Mrs. Martin was a good friend of her Momma's, and her son, Austin, was Deloris' good friend. It would only be polite to stop in and say hello. Even Momma would approve.

While she was in high school, Deloris helped Mrs. Martin by covering the switchboard some evenings when Mrs. Martin had errands to run or tend to her sick daughter. That experience was how Deloris got the job at the KCPD switchboard in Kansas City, and she knew that a telephone operator was the first to know when anything was happening. As she opened the door to the building, she could hear Mrs. Martin say, "How may I help you? Number, please?"

Deloris waited until the call was connected before walking over to the switchboard.

Mrs. Martin looked up, smiled, and said, "Why, Deloris! How are you, dear?"

"I'm fine, Mrs. Martin. How are you?" Deloris replied, smiling back.

"Oh, you know. At my age, if it isn't hurting, I wouldn't know if I was still alive," she said with a wink. "How is your mother?"

"Oh, she's fine. Are you going to the picnic tonight? Momma will be there."

"Yes, I plan to go for a little while."

"This is a very nice building," Deloris said as she glanced around the room.

"Yes, it is. I just moved in a few weeks ago. It was nice and convenient working from home keeping the little ones with me, but I do have more space here and I don't have a switchboard taking up my entire front room."

"I can see how that is better. Who is watching your baby and toddler now?"

"I have one of the high school girls watching them until school starts, since you and Austin went and graduated, leaving me to find someone else," Mrs. Martin said with another wink. "When school starts next week, I plan to have with Penny Powers watch them."

"How is Penny Powers?"

"She's doing just fine."

"That's good. Mrs. Martin, you'll never believe what I am doing now."

"What is that, dear?"

Deloris leaned closer as if to share a secret. "I work on the switchboard at the Kansas City Police Department!"

"No!" Mrs. Martin laughed.

"Yes, really! Austin got me the job back in June. Didn't he tell you, or didn't my mom mention it?"

"That boy seldom calls and never writes, and I've been so busy with the move here that I haven't had time to talk with your mother," Mrs. Martin said, shaking her head.

"Well, I owe him for getting me in the door, but I really owe you more, because you gave me the experience here when you asked me to cover the switchboard while you ran errands."

"I am so happy for you!" Mrs. Martin turned to face Deloris and patted her arm.

"Thank you. It's nice to be back in Jameson and able to catch up with folks and hear the latest news. Speaking of which, I was wondering what you may have heard on the party lines regarding the Gary Green murder?"

"Oh dear. That is such a mess, them accusing Sarah

PECULIARITIES AT THE PICNIC

Gibbs and her daughter. I overheard a curious conversation about him disappearing years ago, but I can't for the life of me remember who was talking."

"Do you remember if the callers were male or female?"

"No..." Before Mrs. Martin could say more, the switchboard lit up in two or three places and buzzed. She turned to answer the calls and gave Deloris a wave, mouthing the word *sorry*.

Deloris pulled her tablet out of her bag and wrote the information down. She hoped that Mrs. Martin would have a little more time to chat, but the switchboard was going crazy with calls, so Deloris put her tablet away and waved as she left the building.

Mr. Dunn's Grocery Store was next, but she didn't believe he would be much help. He was really old and, people said, a little senile. Even if she got information from him, would it be reliable?

Mr. Simpson's hardware store was next door, and she saw him go inside carrying a box of inventory that a truck had just dropped off, so she decided to stop there and try to talk with him. Because it was a hot summer day, he'd left the inside door open and only closed the screen door, so she opened it with a creak and stepped inside to see Mr. Simpson with his back to her, opening up the box. He was getting a little hard of hearing and wouldn't wear a hearing aid, so when she walked up behind him and said hello, he jumped.

"Good lands, you scared me half to death, young'un," he said in his melodious baritone voice as he readjusted his glasses to see who it was. "Why Deloris Markham? What are you doing sneaking in here like that?"

"I am very sorry, Mr. Simpson. I didn't intend to scare you." Under her breath she added, "I seem to be doing that a lot lately." Smiling innocently, she went on, "I thought you heard me shut the screen door."

"That's okay, young lady. What do you need?" he asked.

"Oh, I, uh... I need to see one of those things taken out of the box?"

"You need a fan belt for a car?" he said quizzically.

"Oh, that isn't what I was looking for."

"Well, what were you looking for?"

Deloris looked around for inspiration, but none came. Then she had a thought.

"I want to look at your shovels."

"My shovels? I just sold one to your father last week."

"I was actually wondering if you keep a record of all the shovels you sell."

"I do, but why would you want to know that?"

"How far back?"

"Well, since I first opened the store in 1900."

"Really? Can I see your record book for 1917?"

"Absolutely not," he replied indignantly. "Are you trying to find something out about the Gary Green murder?"

Deloris' face fell. "Maybe."

"Listen, Missy, you better leave that business to the authorities. They can see my records, if they ask, but you have no business nosing around in them. Besides, that receipt book is in my archives in the basement, and I'm not going to dig it out."

"Oh, okay, Mr. Simpson. Sorry to have bothered you." At that, Deloris slipped out the door, with him watching her leave. Drat, she thought. There's no doubt that Mr. Simpson would tell her father that she'd been asking ques-

PECULIARITIES AT THE PICNIC

tions, but if she was lucky, Dad wouldn't talk to Mr. Simpson until after Deloris was back in Kansas City.

Next to Mr. Simpson's hardware store was the jail and constable's office. The last time Jameson had a constable was in 1920. Nowadays, if there were any problems, folks would just call the Daviess County Sheriff, who had an office over in Gallatin. Because no one was at the jail, it was seldom used either, but, the undertaker's office next door was used regularly. She knew from reading the newspaper that Gary Green's remains were taken there when his body was first discovered before it was sent on for an autopsy.

That was it for the buildings on this side of Main Street, so she continued walking back to the picnic. As she did, she glanced across the street and saw Mrs. Harvey open her shop door and exit, followed by Nellie, Maude, and Lara. She started to walk across, but Mrs. Harvey left up her sign saying closed and re-locked the door. The ladies all parted, walking away from Main Street toward their homes. Well, that was that. Interesting, she thought to herself. She decided she needed to keep an eye on that group.

CHAPTER 9

The Talent Show

Deloris walked back to the picnic to find Mayor Fine up on the bandstand, greeting the attendees. He announced that the Talent Show would start in a few minutes, and if anyone else from the crowd wanted to sign up, they could still do so by seeing his wife, who was seated at a table beside the bandstand.

Clarence came up to Deloris and nudged her.

"Go on DeDe. Sign up."

"I don't have any talents other than writing poetry and dancing the Charleston. You may remember that I got in trouble with Momma when I danced it last year," she scoffed. Also, I don't have one of my poems on me to read. How about you? You could play the juice harp."

"Nah, I don't have it on me."

Deloris looked over to see that their brother, Roy, and his wife, Bert, were also in the crowd. Clarence caught their eye and gestured that they should come over and join them, and when they did, Deloris hugged them both. She started catching up with Bert until Clarence shushed them as the show was starting.

The first contestant sang, "The Old Rugged Cross," accompanied by the woman who played the pump organ at the Baptist Church. The lady mostly sang off key and the organist tried to cover for her by hitting the notes a little longer and louder.

Roy told them he'd helped move the pump organ to the bandstand. He added, "It didn't weigh very much so moving it from the church down the street to the stage wasn't hard, especially using Owen Robertson's 1930 Fordson Model F tractor and the wagon it pulled. Owen always has what's needed for the occasion, from wagons and wheelbarrows to shovels and rakes."

A girl about twelve was next, and she read a poem she wrote about the Statue of Liberty. She was followed by a man who played his saw accompanied by his brother on the juice harp. One person after another climbed the six stairs to the stage and displayed their talents.

The last contestant surprised Deloris, Clarence, and Roy, as their father climbed the stairs to the stage with his fiddle in hand. They gaped at each other as Will Markham, the quiet man of few words, took a seat and raised the instrument to his chin with the bow poised above its strings. In one movement, the first few notes of "Turkey in the Straw" began and people rose from their seats and started to dance. Deloris grabbed Clarence's arm and tried to drag him to the middle of the concrete dance floor as people began swinging to and fro around them.

"No, DeDe. What if Mom sees us?" Clarence said as he brushed her hand from his arm.

Disappointed, Deloris stood there swaying to the music. With the crowd fired up, her father played another song, "The Arkansas Traveler," and then left the stage to thunderous applause, whistles, and shouts. Halfway down the

PECULIARITIES AT THE PICNIC

steps, he saw his wife and, with one glance, he could tell that Nannie wasn't thrilled with this display of dancing and frivolity. Though she liked music, Nannie believed that dancing, along with card playing and drinking, was the devil's merriment, and forbade her family to take part. In an effort to appease her, Will returned to the stage to play one last song, "Amazing Grace."

The crowd started singing along and the hymn came to a peaceful close. Nannie looked happier, and Deloris was thrilled that she stayed to witness this. She often heard her father play the fiddle at home, but never in public before.

Will Markham had been the last entry, so Mr. Fine brought all the contestants back to the stage to have the crowd applaud for their favorite act. At stake was a cash prize of five dollars. In the end, it was down to the man who played his saw and Will Markham. It was close, but Will came out victorious. Deloris and Clarence, wild with excitement, looked over to see their brother, Roy, and his wife Bert were also applauding wildly. The siblings ran to their father to shower him with hugs and congratulatory handshakes. Nannie stood by since, of course, she wouldn't hug him in public. She tried to have a stern look upon her face, but the joy of the moment overtook her and she started smiling, then laughing. She squeezed Will's hand in approval. He offered to buy everyone something from the cookshack with his newfound wealth.

As the family was standing in line at the cookshack, Bert turned to Deloris and asked, "So is Thelma coming up?"

"Yes, she didn't get Thursday off, so she should be here tomorrow night. Austin Martin is bringing her and her girls when he drives up after work."

"That's very neighborly of him," Nannie said. "I'll be

sure to tell Frankie she has a well-brought up boy." Changing the subject, Nannie turned to Bert and told her what to bring for the family dinner after church on Sunday. With their Momma's attention on Bert, Clarence leaned over to Deloris and whispered, "Can you tell Austin's chief that he's a 'well-brought up boy'? I'm sure he'll appreciate that." Deloris snickered.

Soon, the night was over. The carousel rides were turned off and the carnival workers went to their wagons to rest up for the next day. The only lights on were in the cook-shack where the night's volunteers were busy cleaning up. They were lucky to have the lights; Deloris knew most town parks didn't have power, but Jameson splurged a few years ago to get electricity to the park and it helped to increase attendance.

The family said their goodbyes and walked to their cars. None of them were on clean up duty that night, but they would be back early the next day to finish what tonight's volunteers left and prepare everything for the new day. Deloris rode with her father so that her mother could ride with Clarence, since his car was closer to the picnic grounds. It gave Deloris a chance to talk with her father alone.

After they got into the car, she asked, "Dad, what do you think about this murder? Do you think Mrs. Green, I mean Gibbs, is guilty of murdering her husband, or is her daughter?"

"No, I don't think they did it," Will Markham responded.

"Then who do you think did?"

"I don't know, but Gary Green made a lot of enemies. Anyone could'a done it."

"What do you think Clifford meant by getting even with Gary Green?"

"He wouldn't have done anything serious like murder him, if that's what you're implying."

"Oh, I know that," she said quickly. I've never known Clifford to hurt a fly. He's always taken care of the wild animals by leaving food out for them. I even saw him hand feed a squirrel once! I just wish I could find out more about Gary Green."

Deloris gave her father a recap of what everyone had told her thus far, hoping that he might offer her some insight or clue.

"Well, Deloris, maybe you need to look at who is acting the most suspicious. Perhaps it isn't even someone from Jameson. Gary got around and did business all over up here. It could have been anyone and everyone." Will paused for a moment, and then asked, "What are you going to do if you find out it really was Sarah or Lucinda or someone who killed him in self-defense?"

"I don't know. I guess I will just stop there and let the sheriff do what he needs to do."

They rode the rest of the way home in silence, while Deloris pondered this possibility.

CHAPTER 10
Sarah Hawkins Green Gibbs

The next morning, Deloris was up early and helped her mother with breakfast. After the dishes were done and put away, she asked her mother if she could use the iron. "My clothes got a little wrinkled in the bag."

"You know where the iron is," her mother replied, nodding toward the top of the stove where it was kept.

Deloris moved it, and the base it sat upon, to one of the burners to heat, and went to get her clothes. Once she finished ironing them, she went outside to find Clarence.

"There you are. When do you think you can take me to Mrs. Greens', I mean Gibbs' house? I've got to remember to call her Mrs. Gibbs."

"I knew who you meant," Clarence said with a wink. "Let me finish up here and get Clifford set up with what he needs to do today. Then I need to get cleaned up a bit and I'll be ready to go. We can't stay long, though. I need to get back here before I head to the picnic this afternoon. Also, how about we have another driving lesson? You really should learn to drive."

"I know, but it scares me so much. Besides, why do I need to drive if I have you?" Deloris wrinkled her nose.

"You don't have me in the big city," he protested.

"I make do," she said, waving her hand dismissively. "There are buses, taxis, and friends there. Anyway, I'll be up at the house waiting for you."

While she was waiting, Deloris rang up Mrs. Gibbs to confirm that she and Clarence would be there to visit with her about nine o'clock, and Mrs. Gibbs agreed.

Mrs. Gibbs' farm was one mile northeast of Jameson and across 13 Highway from the road to the Markham farm. When they turned on the road leading back to the farmhouse, Deloris could see Oliver Gibbs tending to the horses and getting ready to hitch them up to a hay bailer. The house was an old two-story farmhouse with a door on the second story above the porch, and a little balcony outside that door.

When she and Clarence walked up to the screen door, she could smell fresh coffee brewing and, oh my, was that freshly baked cinnamon rolls?

Mrs. Gibbs answered the door, "Come in, come in. Can I get you a cup of coffee and a cinnamon roll?"

"That does sound delicious," Deloris responded. Clarence had a big smile on his face and eagerly agreed with her.

"Let's go into the kitchen, where we can sit around the table and talk," Mrs. Gibbs offered.

"Yes, that'll be swell," Deloris said. After Mrs. Gibbs had served them coffee and cinnamon rolls, Deloris pulled out her tablet and pencil.

"Tell me about Lucinda," Deloris began. "Have you seen or heard from her in any of the time during the last fourteen years?"

PECULIARITIES AT THE PICNIC

"No, I haven't heard from her, and I don't know where she is. I wish I did, because I miss her so much. Looking down, she fiddled with the folds in her well-worn skirt. I did get a note from her shortly after she left telling me not to worry. She said she'd be okay, but she didn't tell me where she was. The postmark was St. Louis, but that doesn't mean she was staying there, or that someone didn't post it for her."

Deloris felt so sorry for the older woman. Mrs. Gibbs looked so sad. "The postcard is good, though. It means that Lucinda got somewhere safe," Deloris said.

That seemed to snap Mrs. Gibbs out of the sadness a bit and she said, "Yes, well, I call her Cindy," she said fondly. "I raised Cindy to be a good Christian girl. She was always willing to help me around the house and around the farm. Her father wasn't Gary Green. Her father was Jethro Hawkins from Cameron but he died in a farming accident when Cindy was eight years old. Shaking her head, she continued, I married Gary when she was ten. He was a means of providing a roof over our head, although sometimes I was afraid we would lose that. This was his parents' farm, and he liked to gamble. His uncle helped us out a time or two to save the farm, and he helped me when Gary disappeared, but now his uncle is gone. Gary doesn't have any family left alive, except for his sister."

"I'm so sorry for all your loss, Mrs. Gibbs," Deloris said sympathetically. "Do you think his sister will try to get the farm away from you?"

Mrs. Gibbs shook her head. "His sister never had any interest in the farm. She lives in Iowa, in a newer farmhouse and a larger farm than this one, so I doubt she's interested in it at all. She got married and left home as soon as she could. She never got along with Gary. Besides, as Gary's widow, I believe I inherit it first."

"What about Cindy?"

She continued, "Cindy was a good student. She excelled in typing and shorthand, but her favorite class was bookkeeping. Miss Lara Cogswell taught the business classes and took Cindy under her wing to help her master the bookkeeping for the farm. She also did well in math and home economics, but those teachers have either moved away or died."

"What did she like to do after school?" Deloris asked.

"She had one friend she was close to, Cathy Willis, and one boy she was fond of, Amos Conaway. Amos died in the Great War and Cathy married and moved to Bethany."

"Who did Cathy marry?"

"Oh, let's see. She married a boy from Bethany. Let me look." Sarah got up and walked over to a big roll-top desk and raised the lid. She pulled out a letter and carried it back to the table. "Here it is. His name is Silas Narramore."

"I think I met him once," Clarence said. "I think I bought some seed corn off of him."

"Silas Narramore," Deloris repeated as she wrote his name and Cathy's on her tablet. "Thank you, Mrs. Gibbs."

Deloris had an idea and jotted down another quick note. Could Silas Narramore be the man from Bethany who came to town threatening to kill Gary because he owed him money? Maybe Silas had sold Gary seed corn also?

"Can you tell me anything about Silas Narramore?" she asked.

"Not really. I only met him once years ago and haven't seen him since," Mrs. Gibbs replied.

"How about the last time you saw Gary Green?"

"I've played this scenario over and over in my head," she said casually folding her hands in her lap. "It was a Friday.

He came home about three thirty in the afternoon and started complaining because I didn't have supper started. I had been sick in bed all day and got dizzy whenever I tried to get up and walk. School had started that Monday and Cindy was almost home from school. She would have started supper when she got home, because we normally didn't eat until around six o'clock, so three thirty would have been a little early for her to start supper. He and I got into an argument, and he stormed out, jumped in his car, and drove off. He might have met Cindy coming up the path to our house, but I didn't see since I was in bed. The other kids in the school wagon saw him say something to Cindy and act like he was going to hit her. I don't know where he went or what he did. I never saw him again, but I suspect he went to one of the taverns in Pattonsburg. He often did that when he got his paycheck from Mr. Worth at Worth Farms."

"I see," Deloris said thoughtfully as she chewed on the pencil eraser and mulled over what Sarah had said.

Clarence cleared his throat, reminding Deloris that he was sitting next to her. When she looked over at him, he tapped his wristwatch—she needed to wrap this interview up.

"Okay, one more question," Deloris said, looking intently at the older woman. "Do you have any idea who may have murdered your husband?"

She sighed. "I really don't. I know that neither Cindy nor I did it."

"How do you know Cindy didn't do it?" Deloris pressed.

"Cindy was afraid of him. She would have run away from him, which I believe that is exactly what she did, but she couldn't have killed him. She was a good Christian,"

Mrs. GIbbs said defiantly. "I didn't kill him either. If you can clear our names, I will be most grateful to you."

"Thank you, Mrs. Gibbs. You've been very helpful." Pushing her chair back from the table, Deloris added, "I do believe you, and I will help you anyway I can to find the guilty person to clear your and your daughter's names. I hope Cindy is found safe and returns to you."

"Thank you, Deloris. It means a lot to me to have someone who believes me and is truly trying to help Cindy and me." She reached for Deloris' hand and squeezed it tight.

As the group exited the house, they saw Oliver Gibbs walking up to them. He joined Sarah on the porch and put his arm around her waist. As Deloris and Clarence got in the car, they could see that Sarah was filling him in on what went on. When they pulled out, both Sarah and Oliver gave them a big wave.

Out of the blue, about halfway home, Clarence said, "Hey DeDe. How about I teach you how to drive now?"

"Now? Oh Clarence, I don't know. Don't you need to get home? There are too many gadgets and levers for me to remember."

Not listening to her excuses, he insisted, "Here, you take over." He stopped the car and jumped out, waving for Deloris to do the same and get in the driver's seat.

First, she couldn't reach the pedals and had to put her bag behind her back to help her stay forward in the seat. Glaring at Clarence, she pushed in on the clutch and put it in gear, as instructed, then she gave it some gas. Deloris stuck her tongue out as she always did when deep in concentration. The car lurched forward and died. Clarence jumped out and ran around to the driver's side, and Deloris slid over on the seat. He set the throttle and turned the choke a little richer, put it in neutral and turned the key. It started right up. He turned to Deloris and told her she wasn't giving it enough gas and letting out on the clutch too fast. He jogged back to the passenger seat and Deloris slid back to the driver's seat. She tried the whole process again, and the car died again.

"Nope, no. I can't do this. You tried to teach me once before and nothing has changed." Deloris implored him, "Can you please just drive me home?"

Switching back to the passenger seat, when Clarence returned to the driver's seat, Deloris added, "You make it look so easy, but it isn't."

"Okay, DeDe. We'll try it another day."

"No, I don't think that I will ever learn how to drive and, besides, I don't really need to learn when, as I said before, I have you and others to drive me around." She smiled sweetly at her big brother as he put the car in gear and drove off.

CHAPTER 11

Bert's Theory

After their attempt at a driving lesson, Deloris asked Clarence if they had time to drive to Roy and Bert's house. "I just want to stop in for a minute," she insisted, expecting Clarence to refuse. Roy and Bert lived in the opposite direction, on the south side of Jameson, nearer to Gallatin, so her request was really out of the way.

Surprisingly, Clarence agreed. "Sure, why not? I need to get a post driver from Roy, anyway," he said with a shrug.

"I know you wanted to get home."

"Oh that? I just didn't want to stay too long at the Gibbs', and I know you like to drag things out a little." He gave her a knowing winked.

"What are you talking about? I don't ..." Deloris protested as they pulled into Bert and Roy's driveway and Clarence knew he won that dispute by default.

Bert was out in her garden and Roy was out in the field on his tractor when Clarence and Deloris pulled up. Bert waved and went to the house to ring the big bell on the porch that she used to call Roy in for dinner. Roy looked up to see them, stopped the tractor, jumped down, and started walking toward the house. Clarence met him halfway at the fence, where they shook hands and stood talking, one with his foot on the bottom board and the other leaning on the top.

Bert ushered Deloris into the kitchen, where she offered her a glass of tea and they sat at the table. Bert started out with questions about Thelma and the girls, then questions about Deloris' work. Then it was Deloris' turn to ask questions.

"Bert, I've been trying to gather information about Gary Green, Sarah, and Lucinda, but most folks have balked at talking about it. What can you tell me?"

Deloris knew Bert would know most, if not all, of the gossip going around town, and would gladly share it. Roy was Deloris' oldest brother, and while they had a good relationship, he sometimes felt more like an uncle because of their age difference. Bert, though, was a lot younger than Roy and only five years older than Deloris, so she was like a sister to Deloris.

"Well, no one seems to know who really killed Gary Green," she began, "but the Jameson folks don't want to know if it was Lucinda or Sarah. Neither of them deserves to go to jail. Everybody knows how Gary was to them. We just want to leave sleeping dogs lie." Bert waved her hand dismissively.

"I get that, but a man has been murdered and surely people aren't okay knowing that a murderer is in their midst. They could strike again," Deloris pointed out. "Besides, Mrs. Gibbs wants me to try to clear her and Lucinda's names once and for all. So, I think they're both innocent." In an expression of pride, Deloris smoothed her hair back from her face.

PECULIARITIES AT THE PICNIC

"Okay, well, here is what I know." Bert wrapped her hands around her glass of tea and leaned toward Deloris. "Some people thought at the time that Gary Green either kidnapped Lucinda or killed her, so we are relieved to know that he is the dead one. But then, where is Lucinda and why hasn't she shown up? She may be dead as well. Her mother married Oliver Gibbs a week ago, and that has people talking. First, they talked about the two of them living together on the farm and now they are talking about them getting married so quickly after his body was found."

"People will talk no matter what," Deloris commiserated.

Bert continued, "Lucinda's boyfriend, Amos Conaway, disappeared about the same time as Lucinda, but then he came back about three months later to help his parents with their farm. He was heartbroken about Lucinda leaving. He may or may not have killed Gary Green, but he'd never hurt Lucinda."

"Did he know where she was, I wonder?" Deloris mused.

"It was said at the time that he might," Bert said with a nod. "Then he joined the Army in the Great War and was killed in action, so we may never know the answer to that question." She paused. "Old Man Jones knows something, but he isn't talking, which is unusual for him. Or maybe he's just still shook up about finding the skeleton. Then there is Craig Ness," Bert went on, shaking a finger as though to scold him. "Where did he get the money to buy a new tractor? Times are tough up here and the crops are barely supporting families with the drought we've had the past two years. With the depression going on, here he comes with a brand-new tractor. How could he afford to buy it? That is suspicious in itself. But," she sighed, "nobody can think of a reason why Craig would want to murder Gary. Then there's Bart and Corny. *They've* been acting suspiciously, bragging about stumbling upon something when the skeleton was discovered that they say proves Lucinda killed him, but they aren't saying what it is. Someone said that it was a quilt or something like that. *Then*, Sean O'Casey has been complaining since day one about everything and everyone, but suddenly *he* is acting suspiciously happy, helpful and even nice. Why now?" She leaned back in her chair to wait for Deloris' reaction.

"Oh my, that's a lot of things to process," Deloris said, taking out her tablet to write the new information down. She wished she had done that sooner. When she got everything jotted down, she asked, "So, why do you think Amos left for three months?"

Bert tilted her head thoughtfully. "He told his family that he and Lucinda broke up and he just wanted to get her out of his system. He said he hired himself out for tobacco harvest and then came back when harvest was done."

"What do you think now, with all this coming to light?"

"Well, he might have killed Gary Green for abusing his girlfriend or running her off. But if that's what happened, we'll never know, since Amos is dead now. He might have taken off with Lucinda until he thought it was safe to return, but if so, where is she?"

"That is true. Where is Lucinda?" Deloris tapped her pencil on her tablet thoughtfully. "Surely, he would have gotten a message to her that the threat of Gary was gone so she could return to Jameson. Well, carry on," Deloris encouraged her sister-in-law.

Bert indeed had another angle to consider. "Another puzzle now is: where is Gary Green's car? If he has been dead all of these years, what happened to his car? Did the murderer take it? Or Lucinda?"

"That could lead back to the man from Bethany possibly murdering him," Deloris speculated. "He could have taken Gary's car to make up for the money Gary stole."

Bert leaned in again, excitedly. "Oh, and then why did Sarah Green wait so long to get remarried if she killed him? She could have had him declared dead after so many years or even divorced him for abandonment?"

"Mmm, all good points. I need to go back and ask her that question," Deloris said thoughtfully.

It was obvious that Bert had been thinking about these things before Deloris arrived, but before Deloris had time to ask her another question, Clarence and Roy ambled into the house.

"Don't you think we had better head home, DeDe? I need to get my chores done before we head to the picnic," Clarence said.

"Yes, I suppose we had better get on our way. Thank you, Bert. You have been a great help."

At that statement, both Roy and Clarence looked at Bert suspiciously, who merely stuck her nose in the air as she crossed her legs and turned away from their gaze. Then she and Deloris burst out in girlish giggles.

Clarence put his hand on the back of Deloris' chair and asked, "What did you mean about Bert being a great help? What did you and Bert talk about?"

"Oh, we were just talking female stuff, you know?" Bert and Deloris giggled at that remark, knowing that neither man would pursue the subject further. Sure enough, afraid of what any more questions would involve, Clarence dropped the subject. Deloris and Clarence said their good-byes and headed back to the Markham farm.

When they got home, they found their mother busy packing up two more pies and a shawl for later in the evening. Nannie always said that you needed to take something warm to wrap up in because you never knew how chilly a Missouri evening could get.

"Here now, where've you been?" Momma asked.

"Oh, we went to see Bert and Roy," Deloris said, glancing at Clarence, who just grinned and stuffed a sandwich in his mouth. Deloris didn't lie. She just didn't tell Momma the entire truth. What harm could that do?

"I know'd you been up to something. Don't try to fool me. You need to eat a sandwich and git yourself upstairs to get ready. Dad and I'll be goin' in early to work the cookshack." Nannie cautioned, as she motioned toward a stack of sandwiches on a platter on the table.

"Okay, Momma," Deloris replied.

"Or you can ride in with me," offered Clarence, "once I'm done with chores."

"That would be great, Clarence," Deloris said. It would give her some time to look through her notes and think about everything that Bert told her.

"Okay, well, I guess we'll see the two of you there."

"Okay, Momma."

CHAPTER 12
Bart and Corny

By the time Deloris and Clarence made it to the picnic grounds, it was nearly six o'clock. Once she'd finished going through her notes, Deloris had been like a child at Christmas trying to hurry Clarence along. Clarence, of course, had deliberately slowed down his chores just to annoy her. Deloris could see the lights from the picnic a mile away, and it only added to her anxiety to get there an hour ago. All the close parking spaces were taken, and they had to park at the end of Main Street across from Ma Roberts' Restaurant.

As Deloris and Clarence walked the three blocks of Main Street to the picnic grounds, they passed Robertson's Mercantile and Millinery, where Nellie Robertson was hanging a handwritten sign on the door that said: Closed for the Picnic. Nellie waved at the Markham siblings as she locked the door and then disappeared into the back of the store again without saying a word to them. Deloris found her behavior peculiar lately. She'd known Mrs. Robertson all her life, and she'd never known her to act this oddly. One minute she was hiding in her shop and the next she was friendly. Then she was having a secret conclave with Maude Fine, Lara Cogswell, and Moira Harvey. She seemed to be avoiding Deloris, maybe because she, like Momma, disapproved of Deloris' questions about Gary Green.

On the next block, they passed the Robertsons' home. Their house was large—not as large as the Fines' house—but a white two-story with a big wraparound front porch. As expected, it looked deserted, with Nellie in the store and Owen, her husband, probably at the picnic preparing for one contest or another at the games.

Next door to the Robertsons's house was the teacher, Lara Cogswell's house. It looked so quaint and cozy with flowers, plants, and a rock garden in the front, and statuary on either side of the walkway to her front door. The two-story frame house had a covered porch that protected anyone standing at the door from the rain. The front door was framed by a porch swing on the left and a bay window on the right. It was a shame that school districts in the early 1900s frowned upon women teachers marrying, Deloris thought. Otherwise, she could have been married with children long ago. She was still a comely woman in her forties.

Behind Lara's and the Robertsons' houses, you could see the back of Tom and Maude Fine's house that faced the next street over. There was no alley, but there was a trellis, shrubbery, and a wooden gate that separated the Fines' backyard from Lara's property.

"Hurry up, DeDe. Momma and Dad are waiting for us," Clarence urged, snapping Deloris back to reality as they walked up to the picnic grounds. "You were in a hurry to get here just a minute ago."

"All right, all right. I'm coming." Deloris had slowed her

pace to admire the houses and their flower gardens, but she hurried now, anxious again to get to the picnic.

As they reached the park, Deloris could see that the band was setting up their equipment on the bandstand. She had never seen or heard of this band before—The Melody Tones. They were from St. Louis and she didn't know what kind of music they played, but she hoped they could get the place jumping, because she was ready to blow off some steam. Walking over to the cookshack, she saw her mother busy cooking hamburgers and her dad selling and serving the food in front. Just last year, she had been helping them by running errands when needed. She felt a touch of guilt by not helping now, but she had signed up to help tomorrow morning during the parade. If enough people were dancing, she could bury herself in the middle without Momma seeing her, and besides, Momma would be busy in the cookshack.

Someone tapped her on the shoulder, and Clarence laughed when she yelped and whirled around to face the person who had stealthily crept up on her.

"Oh hello, Alfie. You scared me half to death! How's tricks?"

"Shall we walk?" was Alfie's response, which was rather mysterious because she was looking around when she said it. Deloris shooed Clarence away towards a group of his friends and then linked her arm in Alfie's. Before they'd gotten very far, Alfie said, "Deloris, I thought you should know that I overheard Bart and Corny just now saying that they were planning to go to Mrs. Gibbs' house tonight after the drawing and get the truth out of her about Lucinda and Gary."

"Oh no. That can't be good. Have you told anyone else?"

"No."

"We need to tell the sheriff," Deloris said as she looked around for him. The good thing about the picnic is that everyone, including the Daviess County Sheriff, was there. "Look, there he is!" Deloris said, relieved as she spotted his uniform near the carousel. She and Alfie quickly walked over to him.

"Excuse me, Sheriff, we need to talk with you somewhere private," Deloris said, catching his attention.

Surprised, the sheriff replied, "How's that?"

"We need to tell you something of great importance," Deloris insisted. "In private."

"Okay, how about we go to um...?" he said as he looked around for a spot to talk.

"Oh, how about my parent's store? It is just down the street and closed now. I have a key," Alfie piped up as she dug in her purse to retrieve the key.

"Perfect." Deloris agreed, and the three walked away from the picnic.

Once inside the store, the sheriff said, "Okay, what's going on that is so important you needed to pull me away from the picnic?" Deloris thought his attitude was condescending, but she was sure that would change once he heard what the girls had to say.

Deloris started, "My friend Alfie here overheard some guys threatening to harass Sarah Green Gibbs, and who knows what else they have in mind? We are concerned that someone will get hurt."

"Is that right?" the sheriff asked, turning to Alfie for confirmation.

"Yes," Alfie replied nervously, fiddling with a button on her blouse. Deloris suspected Alfie had never talked with an officer of the law before and she was intimidated.

PECULIARITIES AT THE PICNIC

"Who made the threat?"

"Bartholomew Shaw and Cornelius Higgins. Bart and Corny," Alfie managed to choke out.

A look of concern crossed the officer's face as he pulled out a small notepad and wrote their names on it, plus some other information.

"And where did you overhear this?" he asked.

"In the parking lot, just a few minutes ago. I went back to my parents' car to get a folding chair and overheard them talking in Bart's jalopy. They were saying they were gonna go over to her house tonight and force her into confessing to the murder."

"And what's your names?"

"I'm Deloris Markham and this is Alphia Thompson," Deloris answered forthrightly, while Alfie nodded in agreement.

"Okay, you girls go back to the picnic, and I'll keep an eye on them."

Then the sheriff walked out of the door, leaving the girls standing there. Deloris and Alfie waited until he was out of sight before heading back to the picnic grounds so if Bart and Corny saw them, they wouldn't suspect that Deloris and Alfie told the sheriff anything.

CHAPTER 13
Friday Night at the Picnic

Back at the picnic, Alfie and Deloris found the band had started to play, but the crowd, mostly seated around in folding chairs and on benches, wasn't into the music yet. Other attendees were either seated inside the cookshack eating or standing around it talking with old friends and neighbors. The young people were walking around the carnival grounds, getting on rides or participating in the games of chance to win a teddy bear or other prize.

Deloris was in the mood for some music, so she and Alfie planned to sit near the bandstand. As they were making their way to the bandstand, they found Thelma, Bert, and Roy in the back of the crowd talking to Dr. David Kerns, Roy's high school classmate and best friend. David was one of Jameson's success stories, having gone to medical school in Kansas City and just graduated in May. His mother moved to the city to be near him, and he lived with her while he was going to school. Now that he finished his studies, he was staying in Kansas City and starting his practice. Roy had asked him to keep an eye on his little sister when Deloris moved there. That annoyed Deloris, but she'd actually only bumped into David once, and he bought her lunch on that occasion, so she couldn't really complain.

As everyone was chatting, the band finished its first song, and the lead guitarist motioned to a woman standing in the shadows at the side of the bandstand. She walked to the center of the stage and started singing. A few, and then more and more, people in the crowd stopped what they were doing and turned to watch who was singing. They seemed mesmerized by her. The chatter of the crowd became a hushed silence.

Deloris waited for the song to end and then whispered to Thelma, "What's going on? Why is everyone so quiet?"

"Do you know who the young woman is, up there singing?" Thelma asked.

"No?" Deloris was confused.

"That's Cindy Hawkins," Thelma explained.

Deloris' jaw dropped. "What?!"

"Yes." Thelma's eyes were moistening with tears as she said, "she's still alive."

Deloris was riveted now, watching her, too. She studied Lucinda's face and her body movements. She could tell that Lucinda was nervous and trying not to get emotional.

Then Deloris turned abruptly, searching the mass of humanity for Sarah Gibbs. Mrs. Gibbs was sitting on a bench at the cookshack eating, and had her back to the stage. Something about the next song, or maybe Lucinda's voice, made her turn around slowly. When she did, she almost choked at what she saw. She stood up and started walking toward the stage, staring at her daughter—now a woman of thirty. As Mrs. Gibbs moved closer, Lucinda choked up and stopped singing. Two guys on the stage lowered her down to the ground and into her mother's arms.

PECULIARITIES AT THE PICNIC

Immediately, the crowd erupted in applause. Lucinda was finally home.

The guitarist from the band stepped up and took her place on the stage and asked the crowd for one more round of applause for the little lady, and the crowd accommodated. The mother/daughter duo walked past the folks who were staring and crying, then past the cookshack and the dunking tank into the street. The crowd seemed momentarily stunned to have just witnessed the reunion. The guitarist announced the band decided to take a fifteen-minute break to give everyone time to soak in the recent developments, and then he would call a square dance when they returned.

Oliver Gibbs ran to get their car and picked up Sarah and Cindy in the street, and the entire crowd watched as the car holding the three of them headed north out of town to their farm. It was only after the dust from the car could no longer be seen that the crowd came out of their mesmerized state, and clusters of groups formed to discuss what had just happened.

Deloris turned to Bert and said, "What do you think of that?"

"It's about time," was all that she said.

Then Deloris remembered Bart and Corny, and regretted not warning Mrs. Gibbs first, before telling the sheriff. She crossed her fingers and hoped that Bart and Corney would have second thoughts and not ruin the joyous reunion. Deloris looked around and caught her breath when she saw Bart and Corny quickly walking out of the fairgrounds, but then she saw one of the sheriff's deputies follow them. She believed the situation would be resolved, and she breathed a little easier.

Alfie followed Deloris' gaze and said, "The sheriff listened. Good."

Deloris nodded and suggested that they go for a walk until the square dance started. The two friends headed toward the carnival midway and ran into two of their classmates. They stopped to chat and then continued walking around past the Ferris wheel, the merry-go-round, and the swings.

Deloris spotted Austin Martin standing near a tent with a ring toss game, talking to one of his classmates. She and Alfie made a beeline to where he was standing. When he saw Deloris, he smiled and waved.

"Well, hello Alfie. Hey there DeDe, I see you made it up here, too."

"Did everything go smoothly with Thelma and the girls?" Deloris asked.

"Everything went right as rain. They're over by the cookshack, talking to your folks."

"Yes, I talked with Thelma. Thank you again for bringing them."

"It was nice to have someone keep me company on the drive," Austin said. "And what have you been up to since you got here?" With one raised eyebrow, Austin looked at Deloris suspiciously.

"I've just been talking to folks," she replied with a gleam in her eye, smiling a little too widely. It was the truth, after all.

"Of course you have," he said in a matter-of-fact tone, nodding. "I suppose you've already found the murderer of Gary Green and the sheriff can relax because you are on the case," Austin said, half laughing.

"I know who it wasn't," she said crisply.

"Oh really? Tell me, who is innocent?"

"Mrs. Gibbs and her daughter, Lucinda!" Deloris said triumphantly.

Austin's eyes narrowed. "Who?"

"Oh right. You wouldn't know that Sara Green married her hired hand, Oliver Gibbs, about a week ago, and is now Mrs. Gibbs."

"Interesting," was all that Austin said.

Deloris continued, "Look at it this way. If Lucinda was guilty, why would she return to Jameson now? You saw her on the stage, right?" Alfie nudged Deloris in the side, but Deloris ignored it, intent on persuading Austin.

"Yes, I did, but that doesn't necessarily mean she's innocent," Austin replied.

Alfie nudged her again, and Deloris ignored her again, because she really wanted to share everything with Austin. "If Sarah was guilty, why would she stay here? Why wouldn't she sell out and leave?"

Before Austin could respond, Liam O'Casey came up to them and asked Deloris to dance. Deloris realized Alfie had been trying to warn her about Liam's approach, and she kicked herself for not paying attention. He was the last person she wanted to see right now.

"Well, um, okay," Deloris responded, wincing internally. She'd broken up with Liam before she'd moved to Kansas City, and while she figured a dance wouldn't hurt, she looked back at Austin, because she had hoped to tell him more and get his take on everything. "We'll talk more later," she told Austin, and he nodded. Deloris took Liam's arm and turned to Alfie, asking her pointedly, "Please keep an eye out for my Momma—she's in the cookshack—and wave at me if you see her looking my way."

"Of course," Alfie replied with a knowing half-smile.

Deloris and Liam walked toward the dance floor while

Alfie found a post halfway between the concrete dance floor and the cookshack.

Austin watched them for a long moment before resuming his conversation with his classmate.

Deloris took a quick glance at the people around the bandstand, checking for her Momma, because she didn't want to anger her again this year. She didn't see her, and Alfie, on the side of the dance floor, gave her a thumbs up, meaning that Momma was still cooking with her back to the bandstand. So, she took Liam's hand and stepped out on the dance floor with the other couples lining up for the square dance.

Deloris looked up at Liam. In high school, Deloris went steady with him, but he got too serious and tried to control her, so she broke it off with him right before they graduated. She'd hoped he'd forget her, but it didn't look that way. Oh well, what harm could come from one dance?

CHAPTER 14
The Dance

Deloris and Liam entered the dance floor where groups of four couples were squared off preparing for the square dance. They found an opening in one group and waited for the music to start and the commands from the caller. The band started playing "Cotton-Eyed Joe," and Liam twirled her around. As they started to dance, Liam leaned in and asked, "Are you seeing anyone in Kansas City?"

"That's none of your beeswax," Deloris hissed. As they Do-Si-Doed and Allemande left, she looked over at the cookshack to see her father sitting and watching her. Where was her mother? Deloris looked around anxiously. She almost missed a step, but managed to keep up. Finally, she saw her spotter, Alfie, in the crowd, who gave her another thumbs up.

When Liam tried to swing her and pull her in tight, she pushed him away to a respectable distance. Over his shoulder, Deloris noticed her father working his way through the crowd, not happy with Liam, either, but Deloris waved him off. She didn't want to cause a scene and draw her mother's attention. The dance would be over soon enough.

The caller directed them to "Promenade with your partner," which meant that Liam held Deloris' hands as they walked counterclockwise in time to the music. That gave him a chance to talk again, and he said, "You should move back here and marry me like you were supposed to."

"I enjoy living in Kansas City and I'm in no hurry to get married, Liam."

"You need to come back here. Don't you care about my happiness?"

"Don't you care about mine?" Deloris shot back. She was really starting to get angry with Liam, and by the look on his face, he wasn't too happy either.

The dance ended and Deloris tried to pull away, but Liam wouldn't let go of her hand, forcing her to stay on the dance floor.

The bandleader announced that "Little Brown Jug" would be the next song, and the music started again. Liam tried to pull her close again, when a really cute guy with sandy hair and sparkling green eyes intercepted her in the "Change Your Partners" command. Somehow, this fellow succeeded in dancing them to another group and Liam was left partnering with Old Mrs. Phillips. The new fellow was a good dancer and Deloris enjoyed herself for the rest of the song.

On the third dance, the new fellow asked Deloris to dance with him again before Liam could get over to her to ask. She looked to Alfie for a thumbs-up that her mother was still too busy to see her dancing, then she accepted.

When Liam arrived, he immediately got into the guy's face and told him to buzz off. The fellow smiled and shook his head no. Then Liam pushed him.

Before the guy could return the gesture, Deloris stepped between them, which wasn't easy and probably not smart, but she said, "Liam, I want to dance with..." she paused, looking at the fellow to add his name.

He obliged, "Les Wells."

"Liam, I want to dance with Les Wells," she said as she nodded toward the fellow. "Back off!"

Liam stood there with his fists still clenched as the band was getting ready to play again, so Deloris got up in his face and said, "I said, I want to dance with him. You need to shuffle off to Buffalo." When he still didn't move, she continued, "Liam, go sit down."

Liam's gaze shifted to Deloris' face, and it was as if he snapped out of a trance. He dropped his hands and said, "All right, but I get the next dance."

"No, Liam, you don't," Deloris replied. "We're done."

Deloris had a look of fortitude on her face and Liam eventually walked away, looking over his shoulder and glowering at the couple, who took their positions in the group.

Everyone on the dance floor was staring at the encounter and Deloris saw her mother turning to look, but Nannie hadn't seen her daughter yet. So, Deloris ducked behind a tall couple who stood between her and the cookshack. Deloris' father, who had made it to the edge of the dance floor, started walking behind Liam, basically escorting him away from his daughter and out to the parked cars.

Deloris turned toward Les and said, "I'm sorry about Liam. He's usually nicer, but he can be stubborn and he's got a rotten temper when things don't go his way. He's a two-headed boy, and they amputated the head with brains."

Smiling, Les replied, "I just don't think anybody should treat a woman like that. No matter how cross they are."

JULIET E. SIDONIE

Deloris looked more intently at Les after that comment and wanted to hug him, but the dance took them apart from each other for a Weave the Ring. When she was by his side again, she felt the need to explain her former relationship with Liam. "He wanted me to marry him after we graduated high school. I liked going steady with him, but I didn't love him. I wanted to see the world before I settled down with someone."

"He seemed to think you two were still together."

"I broke up with him last spring and moved away," she said. The song ended, and Les offered her his arm as they exited the dance floor on the opposite side from where Liam was standing beside his car.

"You don't live around here?" Les asked as they stood at the edge of the dance floor, watching the other dancers.

"Not anymore. I live in Kansas City. Where do you live? I don't think I've seen you before."

"No, you haven't or I would remember you," he said with a grin. "I live in Independence."

"Really? What do you do there?"

"I work at Polly's Pop as the soda pop production manager."

"I love Polly's Pop; grape is my favorite flavor. In fact, I just had one at Mr. Whitestone's cafe!"

"What do you do in the city?" he asked.

"I work for the Kansas City Police Department." Again, she didn't see a need to add that it was for the switchboard.

A look of surprise crossed his face, and then he smiled. "Well, I'd better behave then, hadn't I?"

"Yes, you should, or you might meet my brothers and father in the back forty," she said laughingly. "Why did you come to the Jameson picnic, anyway?"

PECULIARITIES AT THE PICNIC

"I've got relatives in Altamont and they invited me to come up and meet them here."

The next dance was the Schottische, and Les invited her to dance again. They joined hands, skipping, hopping, and twirling around the floor. Deloris, out of breath and laughing, took her final twirl on the dance floor with Les. All the dancing couples applauded the band, and Les leaned in close to Deloris, asking in a low voice, "Would you like to go for a drive?"

Before Deloris could respond, Clarence put his hand on her shoulder and glared at Les. "We're headin' home," he said, taking Deloris' arm and hustling her away from the bandstand.

"But they haven't had the drawing yet," she begged.

"No need to stay. Neither one of us will win. We never do," Clarence asserted. Then added, "Anyway, Mom heard you was dancing, so you'd better skedaddle before she finds you."

The siblings left the park and headed for Clarence's car.

Deloris got into the front seat, crossed her arms, and pouted. "It's a nice night for a drive," she observed.

Clarence smiled and tried to ruffle her hair, though she dodged the attempt with ease. "I'll take you for a drive, anywhere you'd like, and let you drive again," he said with a wink. "Besides, we have a busy day tomorrow," he offered. Deloris rolled her eyes and looked away pointedly, but as she stared out the window, her annoyance with Clarence's teasing quickly shifted to curiosity.

"Clarence," she said, "do you see that truck?"

Clarence looked, and after a second said, "That's Emmett's old pickup truck." He reached over to the door handle, preparing to open it, but Deloris whispered, "Stop!"

CHAPTER 15
The Back Roads

Clarence looked at her in consternation. "Deloris, I don't know why Emmet's driving around without no headlights, but somebody needs to go tell him he'd better sleep it off 'fore he smashes up into a tree."

"But the driver isn't drunk, that's the thing," Deloris explained. "They're sneaking around deliberately." She pointed toward the scene. "Look, he just stopped again and ducked down so that oncoming vehicle wouldn't see him... and now he's driving away, straight as an arrow. He's not sozzled. He's up to something."

Clarence looked at her. "You know, maybe the reason you ain't married is cause you got a suspicious mind."

"No," Deloris replied, "the reason I'm not married is because I've got an overly protective brother who butts in where he doesn't belong!"

Clarence grinned. "You might be right, at protective, but I belong wherever you are."

"Please, let's follow him, at a distance, and keep your lights off," Deloris said. "You did offer to take me for a drive."

Clarence shrugged, started the car, and slowly headed off down Second Street toward Highway 13. Crossing the highway onto P Highway, Emmett was going out into the countryside and still driving with no lights on his pickup truck. Two miles down the road, he stopped at the elderly Mrs. Phillips' house, who must have made it home from the picnic now since her lights were on in the kitchen. Emmett looked around, got out of his truck, and grabbed what looked like two bottles from the bed of his truck. Once Emmett stopped, Clarence had to back up to find a cornfield with a pull off to prevent being seen, which made it harder for him and Deloris to see what Emmett was doing. So, they got out of the car and walked to the edge of the field to get a closer look. They could see Emmett walking to her back door and knocking. Mrs. Phillips didn't turn on her back porch light, leaving Emmett in the dark. They could make out that he handed her the bottles, and they assumed she handed him money back. He backed out of her driveway and started driving back toward where Clarence and Deloris were parked. They waited until he passed and then ran back to their car and jumped in. Clarence quickly started the car but didn't turn his lights on either. The full moon was bright enough to light the road.

"You don't suppose he is selling illegal booze, do you?" Deloris asked.

"With Prohibition in full force, all kinds of nefarious activities go on under cover of night, I've heard."

While Clarence carefully drove, Deloris kept a close watch on the pickup. She could see that Emmett turned right onto Highway 13. Luckily, he never thought to turn back to check if anyone was following him because that large full moon illuminated everything, making it easy for

Deloris and Clarence to see Emmett's truck and movements.

"Hurry up, Clarence. We're losing him!"

"I'm driving as fast as I dare to drive without giving us away to him. Look, he's slowing down and stopping."

Emmett made two stops on Highway 13 headed north, then did a loop turning left on Oak Street and stopped at Alfie's grandmother's house. He carried two bottles to her back door. Deloris liked Alfie's Grandma Thompson. She was always so much fun, such a free spirit. Once upon a time, Deloris and Alfie stayed all night at her grandmother's house when she hosted a pitch party, and the ladies, including Mrs. Phillips, did get a little loud and giggly. Every Saturday night, one of them hosted the group, Grandma Thompson told her and Alfie. She wondered if this delivery was for next week's party.

From there, Emmett continued down the road, stopping at Sean O'Casey's house. Clarence stopped in the shadows behind a hay wagon that was parked along the road and turned off his car. Again, Deloris and Clarence got out of the car and crept to the side of the wagon to watch. Emmett jumped out of his truck again, walked around to the back, and picked up a wooden box filled with bottles that they could hear rattling as he moved it. He looked around and went to the back of Sean's house, where he knocked on the back door.

Sean came to the back door and like Mrs. Phillips, he didn't turn his back porch light on, leaving Emmett in the dark. He took the box and handed him something. Then Emmett returned to his truck and continued on down Oak Street, heading south. He turned left on Fourth Street and finished up at Nellie and Owen Robertson's house. Once they handed him something that looked like money, he hopped in his truck and headed south out of town towards his house. When Clarence and Deloris arrived at Emmett's house, they could see him unloading empty boxes from the back of his truck. Deloris hopped out of Clarence's car before it came to a complete stop and strode over to Emmett, startling him.

Looking around nervously, he said, "Why, Deloris! What are you doing here?"

Clarence caught up with Deloris and interjected, "Hey Emmett, can I give you a hand? We were just driving by and saw you working here."

"Oh yeah," Emmett gave a nervous laugh. "I uh nah, I don't need no help. Thank ya tho. I was jest needun to get these things put away fer mornin. I stayed too long at the picnic, helpin them clean up."

"Mr. Jones," Deloris proceeded forward, trying to look into the boxes, "we saw you delivering bottles to folks."

He eyed her suspiciously. "Oh that. Well, uh. I was uh..."

Clarence spoke up, "You might as well 'fess up. You know she won't stop until you do."

"Yeah, well. Yer catched me makin' deliveries of my cure-all elixir."

"You mean moonshine? Do you have a still, Mr. Jones?" Deloris exclaimed.

"Shhh, not so loud!" Emmett hissed, looking around cautiously.

Glancing around herself, Deloris lowered her voice, but said, "Who's going to hear us out here? A coyote?"

"Them gov'ment folks have spies everywhere. You never know where they may pop up."

"Clarence can keep a lookout." With no hesitation, she went on, "Can I see your still?"

PECULIARITIES AT THE PICNIC

"DeDe!" Clarence chided.

"What? I always wanted to see a real still. I promise I won't tell on you, Mr. Jones."

Hesitantly, Emmett agreed to show her. He led Deloris with Clarence following, behind his house down the hill, about thirty feet to where they could see the Grand River below. In the middle of a patch of trees was a lean-to shed. It was hidden from the river by the trees and further protected from the view of the house by the heavy underbrush. Emmett walked over to the brush and pulled some of it away, uncovering a still.

"I had no idea you were doing this," Clarence said admiringly.

"Yeah, I've been doing this for nigh on five years. I took it over when Old Man Willis died. Took his customers too." Emmett said with a twinkle in his eye.

"Are you sure you don't want any help?" Clarence offered again.

"Nah, I'm almost finished putting everything away," he said as the threesome returned to his driveway. When they got back to the house, Deloris started snooping through a pile of things at the side of the separate garage.

"We'll leave you then. Hope you have a good evening." Clarence tipped his hat to Old Man Jones. "Come on, DeDe. Let's leave the man alone," Clarence scolded as he walked over to Deloris and took her arm, leading her away.

"That's the second time you pulled me away tonight," Deloris said disappointedly once they entered the car.

"You shouldn't make me do it," Clarence retorted.

Back on the road, Deloris spoke up after a few moments of deep thoughts, "It seems funny to hear Old Man Jones call someone else Old Man."

"I know," Clarence agreed, laughing.

"I wonder how old he is?"

"Probably close to grandma's age, I 'spect," Clarence guessed.

"That's old, all right." And they both had a laugh over the development. "By the way, do you have any idea how Craig Ness got the money to buy a new tractor?" Deloris asked. "He was showing it off at the picnic, but I don't know of any farmers that are doing that well this year or for the past three years."

"Craig Ness? We all know that he makes illegal hooch and sells some of it. I guess that puts him in competition with Old Man Jones."

"Really? I had no idea."

Clarence glanced at her. "It's not the sort of thing that you tell your kid sister. I had enough problems keeping you out of trouble in school. You think I was gonna tell you about moonshine? Anyway, there's lots of folks in Daviess County who brew their own. Dang fool Prohibition made folks learn how."

"Huh," Deloris said, a little surprised, and she started wondering which of her friends' parents could possibly be moonshiners. Surely not Mr. and Mrs. Martin. Maybe Mrs. Powers?

"Anyway," Clarence continued, "Craig has also run some illegal gambling games on his property. Mostly they were poker and some betting on the horse races that were announced on the radio, I've heard. Maybe he won a lot of money in a game or sold off a load of hooch?"

"Yeah, but could he have won enough money to buy a brand-new tractor?"

Clarence thought for a second and then shook his head. "Nah, you're right. None of us up here are rich enough to lose a thousand dollars, even if we pooled all of our money together, and that's at least how much he paid for it."

Deloris looked at him and said, "So you're telling me you gamble at the Ness Farm?"

"I didn't say that," Clarence protested.

"If you don't, then how do you know how much you'd all have if you pooled your money together? I bet Momma doesn't know that you gamble. Does Dad?" Clarence looked pained. Deloris laughed and remarked, "I told you I was good at figuring things out."

CHAPTER 16
The Parade

Saturday morning, Deloris got up early, had breakfast, and Clarence took her up to the picnic grounds to work during the parade. Upon arriving, she walked over to the cookshack and asked, "Good morning. Where do you want me to work?"

Moira Harvey was in charge that morning and answered, "How about working the concession stand?"

"That's okay with me," Deloris replied, and took up her post.

The first person in line was Lara Cogswell.

"Hello, how may I help you?" Deloris asked.

Lara smiled a little shyly and said, "How about a piece of pie and a coffee?"

"Which kind of pie would you like? The list is on the chalkboard here," Deloris said as she turned to point at the board hanging up behind her.

"What I'd really like is some of Penny Powers's coconut cream cake, but I know you only have pies?"

"That's true, but you might win it at the cake walk later this morning," Deloris said with a wink. "It smells delectable. I went by the table with the cakes before I started my shift working here." After a moment she snapped her fingers. "Oh, but I heard that Penny also made the coconut cream pie!"

"I would like a piece of coconut cream pie then."

"Coming right up," Deloris responded and turned to the screened-in pie safe on her right. As she opened the door to retrieve a piece of coconut cream pie, she realized the soft pies were in the icebox in the kitchen. She called back to ask the workers in the kitchen to get a slice of coconut cream pie out for her. When they handed her the pie through the curtain, she placed it on the counter in front of Lara. Grabbing a coffee cup from the stack behind her, Deloris filled it with coffee from the coffeepot that sat on a hot plate plugged into the only outlet on the outside of the kitchen.

"Cream and sugar are over there," Deloris said, pointing at the condiment table. "That'll be," she paused as she looked at another chalkboard behind her with the prices, "That'll be fifteen cents."

In line behind Lara was Sean O'Casey. When she turned, she almost walked into him and apologized.

"That's quite all right," he said. More quietly, he added, "I was thinking that we could talk this morning."

Lara Cogswell nodded demurely, coquettishly blushing. Bowing her head, she walked away quickly. Deloris looked up at Mr. O'Casey to take his order, and she noticed a look of longing and love on his face. He paid for a coffee and then quickly turned to watch Lara walk away while Deloris filled his cup.

The next person in line to be served at the cookshack was Dorothy Smith, Deloris' former classmate and the bank teller she had seen working at the Jameson Farmers Bank yesterday.

"Hello, Deloris," Dorothy greeted her. "I'm surprised to see you working the concession stand."

"Hello, Dorothy. Yes, I thought I would help out a little. How are you?"

"I'm fine," she answered softly. "Can I get a piece of cherry pie and a Coke, please?"

"Coming right up," Deloris said cheerily.

She went to the pie safe, opened the screened door, and took out a piece of cherry pie. As she placed the pie and Coke in front of Dorothy, she said leadingly, "Sure was some exciting business with them finding Gary Green's remains, wasn't it?"

"Yes, I guess it was," Dorothy said, but the conversation ended there because she walked away. Dorothy always was a quiet girl, Deloris knew, but she was disappointed that she couldn't even get a few more words out of her.

Out of the corner of her eye, Deloris noticed Maude and Nellie watching her work and putting their heads together, whispering. She caught them saying her name, and though she didn't know for sure, she suspected they were talking about her asking Dorothy questions, or maybe about her going around town yesterday.

There wasn't much she could do about their whispering, so Deloris scanned the crowd to see if there was someone else, she could talk to. She saw Mr. O'Casey and Lara sitting next to each other on a bench and talking. He said something, and she laughed, covering her mouth with a handkerchief. It was cute to watch them. They were like two teenagers flirting with each other. Oh my goodness, Deloris suddenly realized. Sean O'Casey is in love with Lara Cogswell and she appears very fond of him. She wondered why the two had never connected before, but before she could come up with some good reasons, she was interrupted by a flurry of customers.

When the line dwindled because the parade was about to start, Deloris stood toward the back of the concession stand next to the screen that divided it from the kitchen. She overheard the folks in the kitchen talking about Bart and Corny, but she missed the beginning of the conversation and didn't know exactly what they were saying.

The sheriff popped in at that moment to grab a cup of coffee and saw Deloris. "Hey, thank ya kindly for the tip last night about those guys," he said. "We apprehended them standing outside the Gibbs residence yelling and throwing eggs at the house. We took them to the squirrel cage jail in Gallatin to cool off instead of the jail here, since there wasn't anyone here to monitor the inmates. We're waiting to see if the Gibbs want to press charges. They probably won't, but I'm hoping a night in the jail will cool those hotheads off."

Deloris was impressed. "That is good to know. I'm glad that you caught them before they did any actual damage, or worse." She would have asked the sheriff for more details, but then the mayor announced over the loudspeaker that the parade was about to start.

"I gotta go," the sheriff said, gulping the last of his coffee and handing the cup back. "It looks like they're ready to start the parade and I'm leading it. I wouldn't want them to start without me," he said with a wink.

"Thanks, Sheriff."

Deloris moved to the edge of the counter where she could see the parade as it passed by and waited. Looks like the sheriff made it back in time to start the parade, she thought to herself and smiled. He had his siren wailing to get everyone's attention that the parade was starting. Mayor

PECULIARITIES AT THE PICNIC

Fine and Maude followed in their red, 1931 AE5 Chevrolet sedan. On the sides, they had a sign identifying them as the occupants of that vehicle.

Next came a horse-drawn surrey with a sign on the side announcing Doc Graham and his wife, who were seated in it, waving at the crowd. Doc held up his little black bag, pointing at various men in the crowd and laughing. Following them was the banker, Mr. Harvey, and his wife, Moira, in his brand new 1932 Packard. Nellie and Owen Robertson were next in their cream-colored 1930 Chevrolet Roadster. Mr. and Mrs. Simpson followed them in his 1930 Ford pickup. Mr. Simpson had Christmas lights strung around the truck bed that were hooked to a battery, and a sign on the side advertising his hardware store.

The three churches in town each had a horse-drawn wagon decorated with crepe paper, flowers, a cross, and a sign on each side identifying the respective congregations. The parishioners sat around the edges on bales of hay covered in quilts and sheets, followed by a handful of children pulling each other in Red Radio Flyer wagons or on tricycles. Some were walking their dogs or holding their cats.

The Jameson high school boys' and girls' basketball teams were seated in two flatbed wagons, each decorated in the school colors, purple and white, with a picture of the school mascot—a big Siberian husky—towering in the back. The high school marching band followed them.

Various other merchants, politicians, and insurance agents from surrounding towns drove their cars in the parade, as well as bands from high schools in Pattonsburg, Coffey, Jamesport, and Gallatin.

Next came several folks riding horses, all members of the Night Riders horse club. Following the horses were the tractors: a 1923 International Harvester Farmall, a John Deere Model D, and a 1928 Ford Fordson, to name a few, but bringing up the rear was Craig Ness. There he was, sitting atop his shiny, new 1931 red Farmall F-30 tractor, smiling from ear to ear.

Following the tractors was the Jameson Volunteer Fire wagon, with one fellow cranking the horn to make it bellow that the parade was over. With that, it was as if the floodgates opened, and the crowd headed for the cookshack to get some lunch.

Luckily for Deloris, two other people showed up to help at the concession stand and two more came to help in the kitchen. Orders came in for tenderloins, hamburgers, cheeseburgers, and hot dogs. One fryer had tenderloins, and another fryer was for making potato chips, a relatively new delicacy. Soda pop, iced tea, coffee, and ice-cold water were sold, too, not to mention the homemade pies. By the time the lunch rush was over, Deloris was worn out. She was accustomed to serving customers at Poppy's soda fountain, but in this case, she had to learn everything in a matter of minutes, plus watch to see which pies were sold out and which ones weren't. When one of the pies was sold out, she then needed to get a new pie out and cut more slices. It was exhausting, especially because she was trying to listen for any snippets of conversation about the murder at the same time.

CHAPTER 17

Finders Keepers

Tired as she was when her shift at the cookshack was over, Deloris walked over to the bandstand to see the baby show, only to realize that she had missed it. However, her cousins, Mildred and Berniece, were still seated nearby talking to Nannie, so Deloris joined them.

"Did you win?" Deloris asked Mildred, looking at her cousin's child, who was carefully dressed in a pink lace outfit.

"No, this was nap time, and she was pretty cranky," Mildred replied ruefully, stroking the baby's cheek.

"Oh, sorry to hear that. How about you, Berniece?"

"No," she sighed, "he was hungry and crying most of the time."

"That's too bad." Deloris only stayed a minute in order not to miss the tractor pull since she still wanted to track down Craig Ness and ask about his new Farmall.

Saying goodbye to Momma and her cousins, Deloris walked back to the area where the tractor pull was to be held. On her way, she saw Lara Cogswell standing in the circle waiting for the music to start for the cakewalk and gave her a thumbs up. Deloris won a cake a few years ago although Gladys Brown tried to claim it by crowding Deloris off the cake square when the music stopped.

When she arrived at the tractor pull, it was just ending. She quickly scanned the tractors looking for Craig Ness, and spotted him sitting on the tractor seat sideways and talking to a couple of guys. In his hand was a blue ribbon that he must have won in the contest.

She jogged toward the tractor, waving and calling, "Mr. Ness, Mr. Ness!"

He looked down at the young woman calling his name and smiled that same big smile he wore during the parade.

"Yes, can I help you?" he said.

"I couldn't help admiring your new tractor in the parade. My brother wants to get one, but he can't afford it yet. Do you mind if I ask how much you paid for it?" she asked, gesturing toward the large vehicle.

"This baby cost me $1150," Craig answered proudly.

Deloris gave a low whistle. "Wow, how in the world did you afford it in this economy?"

Craig narrowed his eyes and looked suspiciously at Deloris. Then he said laughingly, "The money just fell out of the sky." He looked at the other two guys who were still there and they all started laughing.

Then one of them blurted out, "More like it bubbled up under a tree."

"That doesn't seem likely," Deloris replied disappointedly. "Did you rob a bank?" This comment made the group of men laugh more.

"Not that it's any of your business where I got the money, but I came by it fair and square."

PECULIARITIES AT THE PICNIC

"Did you win it in an illegal gambling game on your property?"

"What?! No." Craig Ness looked a little shocked, but Deloris couldn't tell if it was because he was lying, or because she knew about the gambling. "You guys go on. I'll catch up with you later," he said, waving off the men, who ambled away to look at other tractors. Once they were out of earshot, he turned to Deloris and demanded as he climbed down from his perch on top of the tractor, "Where are you getting these ideas?"

"That's what I've heard people saying," Deloris said with a shrug. "That you can play poker and bet on the races at the Ness Farm."

"Well, could you not go sayin' it out loud in front of everyone?" Craig urged in an exasperated whisper. "The sheriff's around today!"

"I won't say anything more about it if you'll tell me where you got the money," Deloris countered. "What about what your friends said? Did you dig it up?"

"Look, I found it on my property, when I was pulling out stumps. It was buried next to an old tree."

Deloris' eyebrows shot up. "Really?"

"Yes, really."

"Wow, any idea where it came from?"

"No, and I don't want to know. It was buried on my property, so it is mine now. Finders keepers, you know."

"I suppose that would be true without knowing the origins of the money," Deloris replied thoughtfully. Satisfied that he was telling the truth about the money for the tractor, she switched strategies and continued her questioning. "Do you have any idea who may have murdered Gary Green?"

Mr. Ness looked confused at her sudden switch of topics,

but he answered readily enough, "No, and I really don't care who murdered him. He was nothing but bad news everywhere he went. I had my run-ins with him a time or two. I didn't kill him, but I'm glad he's gone and never coming back."

He climbed back up on his tractor and sat heavily upon the seat. He looked down at Deloris and shook his head at her. Then he turned in his seat and started his tractor. Deloris could see that she would not get any more information out of Mr. Ness as his tractor chugged off the picnic grounds, leaving Deloris standing there with even more questions than before.

CHAPTER 18
Lucinda

Deloris crossed through an opening in the trees to Sean O'Casey's property, where the sharpshooter range was set up. There, she found Clarence preparing to take his first shot. She waited patiently and covered her ears as he took aim and fired off three shots. Then the target was changed, and her father came to the mark and took his three shots. The guys running the competition changed the target, then Clarence fired off three more shots, and Will Markham did the same.

Upon close examination by the judges, Clarence beat his father by one sixteenth of an inch in his sixth shot. Otherwise, they both hit five perfect shots through the center and they would have tied. The group of men who were standing around watching and the ones running the competition applauded the young man's success.

His father, with a big grin, shook Clarence's hand and put his other hand on his shoulder, congratulating him. Having finally beaten his father at the sharpshooter competition, Clarence was all smiles. Deloris ran over and started to hug her brother, but settled for a handshake as well. She didn't want to embarrass him in front of the other menfolk. Mr. Peterson from *The Jameson Gem* came up and took a photo of Will and Clarence, promising to put it in the next issue of the paper.

When everything settled down and Clarence had his rifle cleaned, wrapped up, and ready to travel, Deloris asked, "Hey Clarence, can we leave now and go by Mrs. Gibb's house again?"

"Well, I was going to watch the watermelon eating, and nail driving contest, then the sack race, but sure, I guess I can miss them," he said, his curiosity getting the better of him. "What's going on?"

"I want to talk with Lucinda Hawkins and see where she's been and why she stayed away so long. Then see what other information I can garner. I basically only have this weekend to solve this case, so I need to find out as much as I can."

"You do remember that it isn't your case?"

"I know. I know."

"Okay, then we can do that. They are on our way home and I need to go by Clifford's anyway to get some tools I loaned him. Also, I need to see why he wasn't at the end of his road for me to pick him up and bring him with me this morning. I just need to check on him, make sure he's okay, and pick up the tools, so I'll drop you off and go to his place. Let me finish up here and get my trophy."

"Oh dear, I hope he's okay," Deloris said with a frown.

Clarence shrugged. "Yeah, he gets this way occasionally."

"Okay. I'll wait for you by the car." Upon their arrival at the Gibbs farm, Deloris hopped out of the car. Clarence drove off to check on Clifford, and Deloris walked up to the

PECULIARITIES AT THE PICNIC

house and knocked on the door. After a few minutes, Oliver Gibbs came to the door.

"Yes? Oh hello. Deloris, is it?"

"That's right. I was hoping to talk with Mrs. Gibbs and Lucinda, Mr. Gibbs."

From inside, she could hear Mrs. Gibbs say, "It's okay, Oliver. You can let her in."

Deloris smiled a thank you to Mr. Gibbs and walked in to find Mrs. Gibbs and Lucinda seated at their kitchen table with empty dishes from their lunch still in front of them.

Smiling at Deloris, Mrs. Gibbs explained, "Cindy, this is Deloris Markham, Will and Nan Markham's daughter. Oh, and do you remember Thelma Markham? Deloris is her little sister. Remember, I was telling you about Deloris last night? She's the one who wants to help us."

"Oh yes, hi," Lucinda said, looking up at Deloris with a small smile.

"I don't want to intrude on your lunch," Deloris said, gesturing toward the dishes.

"That's quite all right. We were finished," Mrs. Gibbs said. "Have a seat. Can I get you something to eat or drink?" She indicated Deloris should take the empty chair across from Lucinda.

"No, thank you. I don't plan to be here for very long. I just have a few questions to ask Lucinda," Deloris said as she got her tablet and pencil out.

"You can call me Cindy," Lucinda replied, sitting up a little straighter in her chair and listening intently to Deloris.

Deloris didn't hesitate to get right to the point. "First, where have you been, Lucinda...erm...uh, Cindy? And why did you stay away so long?"

"I've been in St. Louis working in a business office for a manufacturing firm there," Cindy explained. "My teacher,

Miss Cogswell, introduced me to her friend who lives in St. Louis, who helped me get a job there."

"I see," Deloris said as she wrote that down in her tablet. "So, Miss Cogswell knew where you were?"

"Yes, I guess so. And," Lucinda paused and looked at her mother, who nodded her approval. "And I didn't know Gary was dead or even missing. I was told not to communicate with anyone back home except to send one letter to Miss Cogswell, signed Grasshopper, our code word, to let her know when I was established in St. Louis. I didn't communicate with anyone else, except ..." her voice trailed off and she looked down at the table.

"Go on," Deloris encouraged.

Lucinda took a deep breath. "I did write one letter to my mother to tell her I was okay, and one to my boyfriend to tell him what happened and to break it off with him." She started crying. "I didn't know that he died in the war until last night."

Sarah put an arm around her daughter's shoulders and pulled her in for a hug. When Lucinda regained her composure, she continued.

"Anyway," she wiped her eyes, "I was told to disappear and not come back for fear that Gary would kill me or my mother. So, I asked Miss Cogswell's friend to mail the letters for me when she went out of town."

"Why would he kill you?"

"Before I ran off, I stole all the money out of his wallet and his precious pocket watch." Lucinda said with a noticeable bitterness in the tone of her voice.

"Oh, I see," Deloris made another note. "But wasn't his watch on him when they found the body?"

"Oh, was it? I don't know. I lost it somewhere on my

way to Miss Cogswell's house." Lucinda dabbed at her nose with a napkin.

"Are you sure you want to go on with this story?" her mother asked.

"I am," Lucinda said with a look determination on her face, as she started her story again. "My stepfather was an ugly drunk. He was always beating my mother and I for any little thing, like if the food was a little cold when he finally came home to eat, or if I hadn't brought in enough logs for the fire."

Lucinda shook her head at the memory, but continued, "That particular day, my mother was sick in bed. Gary came home before I got there from school and, he started yelling at her because supper wasn't ready. He slammed the door and left, which was when I met him in our driveway. Mom told me why he left when I walked in the door. I would have fixed something if I had been home. Anyway, that night I was asleep in my bed. I awoke suddenly to find Gary leering over me, and I was afraid of what he would do next."

Sarah gave a gasp and said, "I am so sorry. I had no idea that he would do that to you." She started crying herself.

"I'm sorry, Mom. I was too ashamed to tell you until now." Lucinda looked over at her mother who was now sobbing, and hugged her. "It's all right, Mom. It was a long time ago, and I survived. He didn't get to touch me."

After a few moments, Deloris asked, "What happened next?"

"I hit him in the head with my alarm clock," Lucinda said indignantly. "Then he slapped me hard across my face and we struggled. I hit him again with the alarm clock, only harder this time, and knocked him out. I was so scared and didn't know what to do, but I knew I had to do it quick before he awoke."

She glanced at her mother again, who had her face buried in her hands, saying "No, no." Lucinda hugged her again before continuing.

"I knew I couldn't stay at the farm anymore, so I grabbed his wallet and took the money, because I knew I would need it to run away. The watch I took out of spite," she said bitterly. "I grabbed my quilt to wrap up in and ran to my mother's room, but she was sound asleep and I couldn't wake her up from her fever, so I gave her a quick kiss on the forehead and ran out of the door. I was barefoot and cut my foot on a rock, but I kept running. When I made it to Miss Cogswell's door, I was so grateful that she was home and let me in. I guess when Gary came to a while later, he took off after me. I don't know why he didn't take his car. If he had, he might have caught Miss Cogswell and me loading her car with a large steamer trunk."

Lucinda started shaking at the memory and her mother gave her a hug this time. "That's all right dear. It's time to get it all out," She said soothingly.

Lucinda continued, "Miss Cogswell told me before this that if I ever needed any help, to come to her and she'd help me; apparently, she already had a plan in place. She knew what kind of man Gary Green was because I guess she went to school with him. I could have asked my boyfriend, Amos, for help, but his family's farm was too far away. Miss Cogswell was closer, so I just ran there."

Deloris nodded in understanding and said, "Go on."

"When I got to her house, there was a light on, and she was still awake. I knocked on the door and she let me inside. She didn't even ask any questions when she saw me, she simply had me come inside. She was getting ready to go on a trip, and she'd just finished packing her bags. That's why she was still up, she told me. She ran and loaded her two bags and asked a friend to watch her house while she was gone, and then she had me help her load the large trunk into the rumble seat of her car. I was to hide in the trunk while she put some books on top, in case Gary pulled up. Luckily, I fit perfectly inside. We took off in her car and I heard her say something about how he was coming up the road as we left town."

"We stayed at a hotel in Gallatin that night. She had me sneak in so the desk clerk wouldn't see me, and the next morning I got into the trunk and we took the train to St. Louis. It was pretty bumpy when the trunk was loaded on and off the train, but I was so glad to be away from Gary, I didn't care. We caught a taxi in St. Louis and went to her friend's house. I can give you her phone number if you need to contact her to verify this."

There was a moment of silence as Deloris thought for a moment, but she said, "I believe you. I'm glad you got away! Do you have any idea who may have killed Gary?"

"I don't know who killed Gary, but it wasn't me," Lucinda insisted. "He was alive the last time I saw him. He was just knocked out. But he was breathing, and Miss Cogswell can affirm that he was running down the road, chasing after me that night." She paused. "I can't say that I am sorry he is dead, though."

"I understand." Turning to Mrs. Gibbs, Deloris asked, "Do you know why he didn't take his car to chase Cindy?"

"No, I haven't seen the car since that day. Or him, for that matter." Mrs. Gibbs replied.

"Why did you marry Oliver only after they found Gary's body?" Deloris pried.

"Well, I couldn't be sure that Gary wouldn't come back

and kill Oliver or me. Then there was also a possibility that I could have been arrested for bigamy."

At that, Oliver spoke up. "I wasn't afraid of him coming back. From everything I heard, he was a no-good coward afraid to fight with men." His face reddened with anger. "I didn't know him or I might have killed him myself."

"Couldn't you have divorced Gary for abandonment?" Deloris asked, continuing to look at Sarah Gibbs, who sighed.

"I could have, but I didn't have enough money to spend for a lawyer and court costs, plus he still could have killed me, divorced or not."

"Oh, yes. Okay. Well," Deloris swallowed hard, "I want to thank all of you for allowing me to ask you these questions and make you revisit the worst times of your life."

"We're grateful to have someone working on our behalf," Sarah said appreciatively. "I don't believe the sheriff is really looking at anyone else."

"I think the information you gave me here will go a long way in finding the killer and taking you off of the sheriff's suspect list." Deloris closed her tablet and put it with her pencil in her bag just as Clarence's arrival was announced by the Gibbs' three dogs as he pulled up outside.

"Sounds like your ride has arrived," Oliver, who was standing near the door, announced.

"Perfect timing," Deloris said as she pushed back her chair and stood up. "Thank you all again for this information. Will I see you at the picnic tonight?"

"I don't know. I suppose you heard what happened last night? I'm not sure the people of Jameson want us there," Sarah said sadly.

"Yes, I heard. That reminds me, though, I do have one

more question. Do you know what Bart and Corny found or why they were coming out here to harass you?"

"I truly don't know. They were yelling something, but I couldn't quite make it out."

Oliver interjected, "I think they were yelling something about Lucinda."

"What they did was absolutely awful," Deloris confirmed. "My friend overheard Bart and Corny talking about doing something and we told the sheriff."

"I am grateful that you did. Thank you." Mrs. Gibbs gave Deloris a hug, as did Lucinda. "It's nice to have someone to talk with who will listen and not judge. You are a good listener."

Deloris smiled at this compliment. "Give the folks of Jameson a chance," she said. "They're not all like Bart and Corny. And some of Lucinda's old friends would love to catch up. I know my sister Thelma would."

CHAPTER 19
Clifford Candy

When Deloris climbed into Clarence's car, he asked, "Well, how did it go in there?"

"I have a lot more information to work with and I think I am close to solving the case."

"You're not going to have them arrested, are you?" Clarence said jokingly.

"No. They definitely didn't do it," Deloris said firmly. "The only thing Lucinda is guilty of is stealing Gary Green's watch and some cash."

Taken aback, Clarence started, "But..."

"I know. The watch was with the body," Deloris nodded. Changing the subject, she asked, "So, what did you learn from Clifford?"

Drawing himself up straight, Clarence announced dramatically, "This is going to crack your case wide open."

Deloris turned to look at Clarence's face to see if he was serious. "Do tell," she said, intrigued.

"I know what Clifford meant when he said that he got even with Gary Green," Clarence said. "But I'm only going to give that information to a sister who doesn't know anything about poker games her big brother might go to."

Deloris rolled her eyes and stuck her tongue out at him. "Come on, you're driving me crazy. Spill the beans. You know I won't tell Momma anything to give her a clue that we are investigating the murder."

"Okay. Well," he paused dramatically. "I know what happened to Gary Green's car."

"Yes?" Deloris demanded.

"Clifford stole his car and hid it in one of the caves on his property. He's had it covered up with old burlap sacks, afraid to tell anyone."

"No!"

"Yes." Clarence nodded.

"How did he steal it?"

"Well, apparently Gary was drunk and on one of his many tirades. He was harassing and hitting him at Mush Evans' garage one night, trying to pick a fight with Clifford, who was just a kid at the time. When Gary went around the back of the building to go to the bathroom, Clifford hid in the rumble seat of his car. Gary went home and left the keys in the ignition. Clifford waited until he thought Gary was asleep inside, and took off with his car. He drove it to his property and hid it in one of the larger caves, where he covered it up with burlap sacks."

"You've got to be kidding me!"

"No, that's what he told me after I followed him into that cave to get some tools that he had borrowed. I saw the burlap sacks and pulled one off, revealing the car."

"He never said anything about it in the past fourteen years?" Deloris said incredulously.

"He mentioned something about a car years ago, but I

didn't think that he had stolen one and had been hiding it in one of his caves."

"What did he say about the car back then?"

"I honestly don't remember now."

"What kind of car is it?"

"A 1916 Model T Ford."

"So, he must have stolen the car the same night that Lucinda left, because she mentioned she was surprised Gary didn't chase her down with his car. Mrs. Gibbs saw the car that day, and it was there when Lucinda got home from school, but must have been gone when Lucinda ran out of the house. Well, that solves the mystery of what happened to Gary Green's car. Thank you for talking to Clifford, Clarence. Look at you being a detective too."

Clarence grimaced at first and then said as he took a small bow, "Happy to help."

Deloris giggled as she pulled out her tablet and pencil. "Well, now to find out who really murdered him. By the way, do you know what Craig Ness told me about how he got the money to buy a new tractor?"

"What did he say?"

"He told me he found the money under a tree when he was digging up stumps. I don't know if he was telling me the truth or not, but I am inclined to believe him. That's too odd to be a lie."

"Legend has it the James gang used to hang around up here," Clarence said thoughtfully. "Maybe they buried money they stole from a bank and he found it."

"That's a possibility," Deloris said as she chewed on the pencil eraser. Then she wrote it down.

When they got home, Deloris found her father busy milking the cows before he got ready to go back to the picnic for the evening's festivities.

"Dad, can I ask you a question?"

"Sure you can, DeDe."

"Clarence told me that the James gang used to hang out up here. Is that true?"

"I've heard that they did. They were up here in Daviess County. In fact, they robbed the Daviess County Savings and Loan in Gallatin."

"Do you think that they may have buried some money that they stole on Craig Ness' farm? I've been trying to find out how he got the money to buy a new tractor."

"Well, you have been talking to a lot of folks, haven't you?" Will Markham said with a chuckle. After thinking for a moment, he continued, "If I recall correctly, Craig Ness' mother married a cousin of Frank and Jesse James, and she used to brag that they stayed at her farm a few times. When she died, Craig inherited the farm, so it could be money that the James Gang stole from the Daviess County Savings and Loan, or from somewhere else, and buried on his property."

"If it was stolen money, that would explain why he has been so secretive about where it came from," Deloris said. She thanked her father and walked away, mulling this information over. Thank goodness Mr. Ness had spilled the beans a little or she never would have guessed.

In her room, she grabbed the tablet and wrote the following list:

1. Talk with Lara Cogswell about Lucinda and the night she ran away. What happened after Lucinda left? Did Lara Cogswell kill Gary Green?

2. Ask Craig Ness if the money he used to buy his tractor was James' gang money.

3. How did Gary Green's watch wind up in the grave with him?

4. Did Amos Conaway have anything to do with Gary Green's death because of what he tried to do to Lucinda since she wrote him about it? Or was he angry because Gary Green ran her off?

5. What did Bart and Corny find in the grave that made them accuse Lucinda?

6. Did the guy from Bethany kill Gary Green?

7. What do Nellie Robertson and Maude Fine know, and why are they so secretive? What do they talk about in Moira Harvey's shop?

8. What does Sean O'Casey know? Why has he changed from grumpy to happy? Yes, Lara is one reason, but is there more to his story?

After writing her list, Deloris freshened up and got ready to go back to the picnic grounds. She went downstairs to find Clarence coming in from his chores.

"I just need to get cleaned up and changed, then I am ready to go back, DeDe," he said. "We might make it back in time for the husband-calling contest. You should be there for that; I hear it's a skill every married lady needs and you might find your future husband there," Clarence nudged her as he walked by.

Deloris stuck her tongue out at her brother.

CHAPTER 20
Cathy Narramore

At the picnic, people were standing in groups or sitting in folding chairs, while the children and teenagers were walking around the carnival games or lining up to ride the amusement rides. Saturday night was the most popular night because everyone was off work and all the folks who'd moved away came home for the picnic, so the crowd was larger than the last two nights.

Deloris was surprised to see Clifford among the crowd when they arrived. He usually avoided large crowds, yet here he was. When Clarence saw him, he walked over to greet him and talk.

Deloris soon found Alfie, and the two wandered around and enjoyed seeing several of their friends. Almost all their classmates were home for the picnic. One girl was missing, and Alfie told Deloris that it was because she was having a baby, which was scandalous because that meant she must have been pregnant when they graduated, and girls weren't allowed to attend school if they were pregnant. A boy from their class was missing, too, and she was told that he was working in Nevada on a dam project on the Colorado River.

When Alfie and Deloris ended up over by the carnival rides, Alfie elbowed Deloris, saying, "Look, there's Liam up on the Ferris wheel."

Deloris groaned. "Mind if we walk back toward the bandstand?" Deloris replied, trying to duck under a tree so that Liam wouldn't see her.

"Not at all," Alfie said, and the two young ladies headed back towards the bandstand. Smiling mischievously, she added, "But maybe that sandy-haired fellow will come find you and rescue you again."

"You mean Les?" Deloris asked, trying to stay nonchalant.

"Is that his name? Well, how is Mr. Les?"

Deloris laughed, and said, "I haven't seen or talked to him since the dance last night."

"I bet Leon, your boyfriend in the city, is heartbroken right now."

Deloris smiled, thinking of the man she occasionally dated in Kansas City. "Leon is so busy repairing everyone's soda machines, and ice cream machines, and freezers and so on, that I've barely seen him." She waved her hand dismissively. "He's a fun date, but we're not going steady. We've never even talked about it."

"Okay. But I have a question for you."

"What?"

"Why are you only attracted to men whose names begin with L?"

Deloris stopped walking. "What are you talking about?"

"Liam. Les. Leon." Alfie counted on her fingers as she listed their names.

"I hadn't even noticed."

"Some detective you are. I predict that the next time

you go on a date, it will be with someone whose name starts with "L," the same letter as love."

Deloris and Alfie both giggled at that. Then Alfie saw her grandmother waving her over, so she said goodbye to Deloris and went over to the older woman.

Deloris continued walking toward the bandstand when Lucinda walked up with a woman of about the same age at her side.

"Hi there, I'd like to introduce you to my best friend, Cathy Narramore. She knows all of my darkest secrets or did." Lucinda looked at Cathy and smiled. "I thought she might help you if you want to know more about Amos Conaway, plus she knew my stepfather. She talked with Amos before he went into the service."

"How do you do, Cathy," Deloris replied, reaching out to shake hands. "I would like to talk with you. Can we step over to the side where there aren't as many people?"

"Sure. What would you like to know?" Cathy asked as they found a quieter spot.

"How was Amos after Lucinda left?"

Lucinda interrupted, "Remember, you can call me Cindy. All my friends do."

"Oh yes, Cindy," Deloris smiled and turned to Cathy for her answer.

"He was very upset," Cathy explained. "At first he was threatening to kill Gary for running Cindy off, because he thought Gary was the reason that Cindy left, had maybe even been the one who took her away, but then when Gary never came back and it looked like they had disappeared together..." She shuddered as her voice trailed off.

"Then what happened?" Deloris prompted.

"Then Amos disappeared for a while. He was really upset and down. He even started drinking, and he had never touched alcohol before. After he came back, he said he'd been working as a hired hand at a tobacco harvest, but he didn't tell his folks that before he left. No one's really sure where he went, or if that's what he actually did. Then he went away and fought in the Great War, and never came back. He told me before he left that he might as well go fight. He didn't really know what to do with himself here with Cindy gone so suddenly and without a goodbye except for her letter with an explanation that made him angry too."

The women looked at each other with pained expressions, and Cathy patted Lucinda's arm.

"That's all I know about Amos. But my husband didn't like Gary Green either," Cathy offered. "Before I met him, Mr. Green cheated my Silas out of some money for a car."

"Oh, your husband must have been the man from Bethany, whom I heard was looking for Gary, threatening to murder him."

"Oh, um. Well, I'm sure he didn't really mean that he would *murder* Mr. Green," Cathy responded, lowering her voice. "He was furious, but he wouldn't kill anyone."

"Would you mind if I talked with your husband?" Deloris asked. "He might shed some light on who killed him."

Cathy hesitated but agreed. "Yes, okay. He's over there talking to my brother." She led Deloris over to her husband, a tall, handsome man with friendly eyes and an easy-going smile. Deloris studied his face while Cathy introduced him. "Silas, this is, uh, I don't believe Cindy said your name."

"Deloris, Deloris Markham," she said, reaching out to shake Silas Narramore's hand. She didn't detect anything sinister about him.

"Oh, are you related to Thelma Markham?" Cathy asked.

PECULIARITIES AT THE PICNIC

"Yes, she is my sister."

"How is she? I haven't seen her for years?"

"She's here somewhere," Deloris said as she looked around for Thelma, but didn't see her, so she continued. "Mr. Narramore..."

"Call me Silas. Mr. Narramore is my father," he interrupted, laughing.

"Okay, Silas," Deloris started again. "I understand that Gary Green cheated you out of some money."

"Yes, he did. I sold him a car, and he never paid me for it," Silas answered, crossing his arms across his chest.

"What kind of car was it?"

"A 1916 Model T Ford."

"I may be able to help you get that car back," Deloris said mysteriously. "Do you have a bill of sale or any paperwork on it to prove that you own or owned it?"

Tilting an eyebrow, Silas said, "I have what the Ford dealer gave me. Meant to throw it away, but I came across it the other day."

"Great. Hang on to it and I'll let you know."

"But how do you have my car? Where is it?

"I think my brother may have found it, but I'll let him talk to you about it. Now, do you have any idea who may have killed Gary Green?"

"No, but I learned after my dealings with him that several people hated him enough to murder him," he scoffed. "I wasn't the first person he cheated."

Just then, some classmates of Lucinda walked up, interrupting their conversation. "Do you mind if we finish this later?" Cathy asked Deloris quietly. "I want to be there for Lucinda if any of these old friends start being mean."

Deloris nodded and turned to Silas, saying, "I may need to ask you about them, and I have some more questions, if you don't mind. Maybe I could talk to you and Cathy more tomorrow?"

"That's fine with me. Cathy can give you directions to our house."

"Thank you," Deloris replied and then turned to Cathy, who told her how to get to their house. Deloris wrote the directions down in her tablet. Then, with the Narramores' support, Lucinda started catching up with her old classmates.

CHAPTER 21
Picnic-Goers

Deloris saw Lara Cogswell sitting with Sean O'Casey on some wooden lawn chairs nearby. They looked so happy enjoying a private conversation in the middle of friends and neighbors. She touched his arm, and he reached for her hand, holding it a little longer than society would approve. Deloris hated to interrupt them, but she needed to get the rest of the story.

Walking up to the couple, she leaned down and asked, "Miss Cogswell, may I speak with you in private?"

"Oh, uh. Okay," she looked at Sean and he nodded.

"Let's go over here behind the bandstand," Deloris offered.

Lara froze. "No, I'd rather go anywhere else but there."

"Oh yes, I understand. How about over at the edge of the picnic grounds?" Lara's uneasiness about going behind the bandstand made Deloris even more curious. "I talked with Lucinda Hawkins earlier today, and she told me that you helped to get her out of town and away from her stepfather."

Hesitantly, Lara responded, "Yes, I did."

"I am trying to figure out how Mr. Green's watch wound up back with his remains and what happened after Lucinda left?"

There was a long silence before Lara answered, "I think we need to talk in a more private setting than this. Can you come by my house tomorrow? I promise I will tell you everything then."

"Yes, I can do that. What time?"

"After church, how about two p.m.?" Lara offered.

"If we can make it two-thirty, I can do that. I have another person I am talking with at one o'clock. My return train to Kansas City leaves at five o'clock. I may try to find a ride back instead."

Lara agreed, and they both returned to the main picnic grounds. Lara sat back down by Sean O'Casey, while Deloris found Austin by the cookshack eating a tenderloin.

"What time are you leaving tomorrow and may I snag a seat?" she asked him.

"We can squeeze you in between the girls in the rumble seat," he said, smirking. "I plan to leave about six o'clock."

"Thank you," Deloris replied, ignoring his remark. "That'll be swell."

As she turned to walk away, she spotted Thelma, Roy, and Bert talking to Dr. David Kerns. A red-headed woman standing next to David in the group must have been his girlfriend from the city. She stopped to say hello to the group and then was off to find Clarence to ask him about taking her to the Narramore's and Miss Cogswell's.

At the far north end of the picnic grounds among the last row of parked vehicles, she found him talking to some of his friends. As she walked over to them, she saw bottles in their hands. It looked like they were drinking some hooch, she thought to herself, but she almost couldn't believe her eyes as she walked closer. She'd never seen her big brother drink anything but coffee, tea, and water. First, he gambled, and now this? When Clarence saw her, he almost choked as he half walked and half ran to meet her part of the way, out of his buddies' earshot.

"Don't tell Mom," he quickly pleaded.

"Oh, Clarence. You're a grown man. You shouldn't worry about Momma, but then you do live with her and Dad," Deloris commented as she put her index finger to her chin in a thoughtful pose.

"Yes, I do, and I don't want any trouble with either of them. I was just trying this stuff out," he reasoned.

"Sure, you were. I believe you," Deloris said sarcastically. "Where'd you get it? Did you get it from Old Man Jones?"

"I might've."

"You did! Clarence!"

"What?"

"Well, I guess then you won't mind running me around tomorrow to a few different places for my silence," Deloris added with a twinkle in her eye, pleased to have information to use to her advantage.

Knowing he was caught in Deloris' scheme, he mumbled, "No, I won't mind. Where are we going? After church and Sunday dinner, right?"

"Yes, of course. I don't want to get into trouble with Momma." She gave Clarence a wink and added, "I need to go to Bethany, then on to Lara Cogswell's house, or vice versa."

"Bethany!"

Deloris nodded and flashed innocent eyes at him.

"All right," he conceded.

"Thanks!" Deloris said triumphantly and turned to go

back to the main picnic ground, where she found Alfie at the edge.

"How was your grandmother?" Deloris asked.

"She's doing well, thanks. Where have you been?"

"I went looking for Clarence."

"Did you find him?"

"Yes, he was with a group of his friends."

"Would you like to try some rides? I haven't seen Liam since the Ferris wheel."

Deloris agreed, hoping that Liam was long gone, but hiding from him at the picnic couldn't last for very long. It wasn't that big of a park. They stopped at the ticket booth and each bought five tickets for ten cents. Walking past the swings, they got in line for the Ferris wheel.

"Let's get on the swings next," Alfie said excitedly.

Just then, Liam O'Casey and another boy came up and stood behind them in line. "Where's your boyfriend?" Liam said with a sneer.

Before Deloris could answer, he continued, "Hey girls, how about we switch partners and get on?"

"No thank you, Liam," Deloris replied firmly. She wasn't too excited about resuming a conversation with Liam, especially after his actions the night before. When she looked at her friend, Alfie was blushing, and Deloris could tell that she was interested in the other boy, so she begrudgingly changed her mind.

They got on the ride in silence, and right away the Ferris wheel stopped at the very top. Liam put his arm around Deloris' shoulders and made a pass at her. She slapped him, then jerked away, making the car swing.

"Listen, Liam. I agreed to sit with you because Alfie likes your friend, but I'm not interested in restarting a relationship with you. I live in the city now and I don't want a long-distance relationship, and if I did, I wouldn't want a relationship with you. I have no feelings for you whatsoever." The words came tumbling out as she wedged herself into the corner of the car, as far away as she could get.

Deflated, Liam removed his arm from around her shoulders and sat back in his seat. "I was going to ask you to dance when we get off of here, but ..."

"Why don't you find someone else to dance with? I'm not the person who will make you happy, Liam. The sooner you understand that, the better," she said, softening a bit.

"I miss you," Liam said. "You were always up to something interesting, and easy to talk to."

"I'm sorry to hurt you, but I need to make it clear. I said no." Deloris looked him straight in the eye.

The next moment, when Deloris looked down, she saw Craig Ness in the carnival area talking to two men. She made a mental note of where he was standing and as soon as the Ferris wheel stopped, she hopped off. Alfie and her seatmate arrived shortly thereafter.

"Sorry, guys, I see someone that I need to talk to right now. Alfie, do you want to come with me or ...?"

"Oh, I'll... uh." Alfie looked at the guy standing next to her.

"That's okay, Alfie. I'll catch you later," Deloris said, turning quickly to walk in the direction of where she saw Craig Ness.

Catching up to him, she asked, "Mr. Ness, may I talk with you?"

"Again? I'm kind of busy here," he said, clearly annoyed.

"It won't take long. I just have a quick question." Deloris smiled as innocently as she could.

"Okay, what do you need, young lady?" he relented.

"Did you really find a bag of money that you used to buy the new tractor? Was it money from one of the James Gang robberies?"

Craig's eyes narrowed as he looked first at Deloris and then at the men he was talking with before. "What? No." Then he turned to the two men and said, "Hey guys, I'll catch up with you later." Then he took Deloris' arm and pulled her to the south edge of the picnic grounds. "Why would you say that?" he demanded.

"Well, I am investigating Gary Green's murder, and I want to rule you out as a suspect."

"Who are you anyway?"

"I am helping the sheriff flush out suspects other than Sarah Gibbs and Lucinda Hawkins," Deloris said firmly, yanking her arm from Craig's grasp.

"Look, I didn't like Gary, but I didn't kill him," he said, voice raising. "I could have killed him when he burned my barn down years ago, but I didn't. The sheriff never could prove he did it, but I know he did."

"I see." Deloris pulled the tablet and pencil out of her purse.

"What are you writing there?" he said, agitated.

"I'm writing that you did have a motive to kill him."

"What! No! As I said before, I didn't like Gary, but I didn't kill him." Craig took his hat off and smoothed his hair before roughly replacing the hat in frustration.

"Where were you the night Gary Green disappeared?" Deloris pushed.

"I don't remember. That was too long ago and besides, I don't know exactly when he disappeared." He threw up his hands. "But if it was the weekend of the Jameson Picnic, I took a load of corn to St. Joseph that Saturday and didn't come home until Monday. There was a drought that year and the corn didn't fill out as much, so it was an early harvest."

Skeptical, Deloris asked, "How do you remember that?"

Pacing a bit, he responded, "Well, the paper said he had been missing for fourteen years and I overheard someone say that it was just after the picnic, so I went home and went through my records to see if I could remember anything. That year, I recorded the sale, so I knew I wasn't in town."

"Okay, so, where did you get the money for your new tractor?"

"Okay, you are right," he admitted, his steps slowing. "I was pulling up tree stumps on my property, like I told you before, when I saw a piece of a carpetbag sticking up. A corner was torn, probably when the stump came up, and out spilled gold coins and paper money. I don't know exactly where it came from, but I suspect it might have been from the James gang. My stepfather was a first cousin to Frank and Jesse and my farm was his farm before my mother married him. I am his sole heir, so it is money I found on my property with no information from where it came. So, finders' keepers," he said defensively.

"Relax, Mr. Ness. I'm only looking for a murderer. I just needed to know if you killed Gary for money. I won't say anything about this to the sheriff. I'll leave it up to you to resolve. Thank you for being honest with me."

At that, Deloris closed her tablet and walked away, thinking to herself, "Well, that's another suspect off of the list." Problem was, she said it halfway out loud.

"What?"

There was Alfie, standing next to a carnival game with a blue and white teddy bear in her arms and a dreamy look in her eyes. The young man had his back to her, preparing to shoot a BB gun at the metal ducks as they moved across the back of the tent.

"Oh, Alfie. It was nothing. I was just thinking out loud. It looks like you have something special there."

"Oh, yes. Isn't he dreamy?" Alfie gazed at her new beau.

"I meant the Teddy bear, but yes, I can see that you have someone special there too," Deloris smiled.

"Oh, did you want to go back to the bandstand?" Alfie asked.

"You stay here. I'll be at the bandstand if you need me." Deloris offered.

Alfie smiled and nodded.

Then, Deloris saw Nellie Robertson, Moira Harvey, and Maude Fine seated in the front row of the crowd waiting for the prize drawings. She saw an opportunity to sit behind them and took it. Luckily, none of them turned around to see who was seated behind them right away. Deloris leaned slightly forward to eavesdrop on their conversation.

"Yes, I know. Can you believe she talked with her?" She overheard Nellie say.

"Well, I can't believe that she ..." Maude turned around at that point and saw Deloris. The look on her face made it seem like she was having a stroke.

"Oh, hello ladies. Don't mind me," Deloris said, leaning back and straightening her skirt.

From the looks on all of their faces, it was obvious that they were talking about her. So, she decided to take advantage of the situation and their embarrassment.

"I've been meaning to talk with all of you. I'm trying to help Mrs. Gibbs and Lucinda Hawkins. May I ask you a few questions?"

"Absolutely not!" Maude said in a huff.

PECULIARITIES AT THE PICNIC

Nellie looked at Maude with eyes like saucers, but Moira was stoic.

"And neither of them has anything to say to you either," Maude quickly added with an authoritative tone.

All three women would have probably left at that point, but the free drawing was about to begin and moving their chairs meant they would need to go to the back of the crowd nearest the carnival rides where it would be harder to hear their names if they were called.

"I don't understand why you are avoiding me and being so secretive," Deloris said.

"Look, dear. We just want to put all of this ugly business about Gary Green behind us and you keep bringing him up," Nellie answered with a slight tremble in her voice.

"I just want to help Mrs. Gibbs and Lucinda, because I don't believe they had anything to do with Gary Green's death. Don't you want to help them?"

"Well, I don't believe the sheriff will find enough evidence to bring either of them up for charges, so they shouldn't need our help," Maude reasoned.

As if on cue, the sheriff appeared with Lucinda, walking past the bandstand and escorting her off the picnic grounds.

"Well, that doesn't appear to be so," Deloris said as she jumped up to follow them.

Maude, Moira and Nellie sat perfectly still, each completely shocked at the sight of the sheriff forcing Lucinda to go with him.

CHAPTER 22
The Sheriff

By the time Deloris caught up to the sheriff and Lucinda, he had her in his car and was backing out of the parking space near the cookshack.

Feeling a sense of urgency, Deloris went to the back parking area to find Clarence. On her way, she ran into Les.

"Hey there, beautiful, where are you going in such a hurry?"

"Oh, hey Les. I'm looking for my brother. I need him to take me somewhere," she said quickly.

"Well, I've got a car. I could take you," Les offered.

"I don't know," she said, standing on her tippy toes to look over the crowd.

"Where do you need to go?"

"The Sheriff's Office."

"Wh-why there? Is something wrong? Did that guy hurt you?" he asked, concerned.

"Oh, Liam? No, he didn't hurt me. The sheriff just arrested a, uh, a friend of mine and I need to help her."

"Okay, well, where is the Sheriff's Office?"

"In Gallatin. I really need to find my brother first before I go," she said, starting to get worried.

"Okay, then I'll help you. What does he look like?"

"He's about this high," she gestured with her hand above her head. "With brown hair and blue-green eyes. He's wearing a white shirt, blue jeans, and a straw hat."

Les looked around and Deloris saw that her description could fit several of the guys in the crowd.

She added, "Oh, you met him last night when you asked me to go on a ride, remember?"

"That was your brother?"

"Yes, one of them. Who did you think it was?"

Les shrugged. "I don't know. Okay, then I'll help you look for him," he said, and he took off into the crowd.

Deloris headed out to where cars were parked four deep, and found Clarence's car near the trees that divided the picnic grounds from Sean O'Casey's field on the other side. Clarence was asleep in the front seat. Deloris leaned over to shake his shoulder to wake him up, and then she smelled the alcohol on his breath.

"Great!" she said out loud to no one in particular. Her brother wasn't asleep, he was passed out. At that moment Les walked up and Deloris said, "I guess I would like to get a ride with you if the offer still stands?"

"It does," he said with a nod.

"I just need to find some of my family and let them know where I'm going."

Les followed Deloris as she hurried back to the cookshack, where she spotted Bert and Roy sitting with Thelma. The three were eating pie and having a big laugh. Deloris walked up behind Bert and cleared her throat. "Hey, guys, I can't find Clarence," she said. Les looked startled, and she gave him a look, hoping he'd stay silent. "I need to go to

PECULIARITIES AT THE PICNIC

Gallatin. Les here offered to take me. I don't know when I'll get back."

Bert, Roy, and Thelma eyed Les suspiciously. "Who is this?" they said in unison.

"This is Les Wells. He is visiting relatives who live in Altamont and came to the picnic to check it out. He's originally from Independence."

"And you just met him here? DeDe, I think you'd better find Clarence," Thelma said.

"I, uh, well, okay, he's asleep in his car. I don't think he's feeling very good. He looked kinda sick."

"You know Momma and Dad left to put the girls to bed," Thelma scolded. "They wouldn't approve."

"I know, but I need to go now."

"Then we'll take you. Where in Gallatin are you going?" Roy offered.

"The Sheriff's Office."

"Why in Hades are you wanting to go there?" Roy blurted out, annoyed.

"Lucinda's been arrested, and I need to see if I can help her."

"DeDe, you need to let her mother help her. Stay out of it," Roy admonished.

Les, listening to this exchange, looked bewildered.

"All right, then I need a ride to her mother's so I can go with *her* to Gallatin." Deloris stomped her foot. "Look, can you take me or not?"

"I'll go with her, if she goes with Les," Bert offered.

"There. Is that okay with you?" Deloris asked Roy, flipping her hands out in front of her.

"I, uh..." Roy knew that he'd lost the battle when his wife took Deloris' side. He looked at Thelma for help and she shrugged, "Okay."

"Are you still okay to take us?" Deloris said, turning to Les.

"Yeah, sure," was his reply. The three of them piled into Les' green 1928 Plymouth coupe and they were off.

On the way to Sarah's farm, Deloris filled Les and Bert in on her investigation. She said to Les, "You didn't know what you were getting yourself into, did you?"

"No, but I like it. I'm intrigued at how this is going to go," Les said as he pushed the accelerator down to speed the car up.

Coming down the road headed in the opposite direction were Sarah and Oliver Gibbs. They were obviously heading to Gallatin, too, so Deloris asked Les to turn the car around and follow them.

Thirty minutes later when they got to the Daviess County jail, Deloris and Bert hopped out of Les' car as he went to park. They burst into the outer office, where they found Sarah and Oliver pleading with the sheriff.

Deloris added to their plea, "Sheriff, you're making a mistake. Lucinda didn't kill Gary Green."

"Look," he replied. "I'm being pressured to close this case, and Lucinda seems the obvious suspect. We found long brown hairs on what was left of Gary's clothes that matches her hair, I've been told, and his remains were wrapped in a quilt. We have confirmation that it belonged to Sarah because her signature was in the left corner. Sarah has, or had, darker hair than was found, so we believe it belongs to Lucinda."

"But she didn't do it," Deloris implored.

"Then who did?" was the sheriff's exasperated response.

At that moment, the door opened and in walked Lara Cogswell and Sean O'Casey.

PECULIARITIES AT THE PICNIC

"Sheriff, I murdered Gary Green. You need to release Lucinda," Lara said more forcefully than anyone had ever heard her speak.

Sean O'Casey looked at her surprised at first, and then said, "No, Sheriff. I killed Gary Green. You need to arrest me."

The sheriff started scratching his head under his hat, when the door opened and in walked Nellie and Owen Robertson.

Nellie blurted out, "Sheriff, I murdered Gary Green. You need to release Lucinda Hawkins. She didn't do it. Arrest me."

Owen looked at his wife and then spoke up, too. "It was me, Sheriff. I killed Gary Green."

Moira and Geoffrey Harvey burst in the door, and Moira exclaimed, "I did it! I slay Gary Green."

Her husband stepped in front of her and said, "No, it wasn't you. It was... me!"

Exasperated, the sheriff yanked off his hat. "Look, I can't arrest all of you," he said. "The jail won't hold you. You people all need to leave."

Before the sheriff could say more, Maude and Tom Fine rushed inside the office, too. Maude was obviously out of breath from running a distance. Deloris surmised that with all the people arriving ahead of them, they obviously had to park farther away.

"Sheriff, I confess. I killed Gary Green," Maude gasped, trying to catch her breath.

Tom then jumped in, "No, I did it, Sheriff. I killed ..."

But he couldn't finish his statement before Emmett "Old Man" Jones opened the door and walked in calmly. Everyone in the Sheriff's Office turned and watched him slowly take off his hat. They parted a path for him as he walked up to the sheriff.

"Sheriff, all these good people need to go home. You see, I killed Gary Green. I did it. I done buried him under the bandstand and forgot I put him there. Arrest me."

The sheriff looked dumbfounded at first, but then stated, "You dern fool. Do you realize you are confessing to murder? And I'm pretty sure you didn't do it!"

"I did it. I tell you," Emmett replied. "Whether you believe me or not, I know'd what I'm doin. Arrest me."

Emmett held out his hands for the sheriff to put the handcuffs on him. When the sheriff refused to do it, Emmett walked over to an empty jail cell, went inside, and pulled the door shut.

"Emmett, you're as crazy as a loon. I can't arrest you without evidence," the sheriff shouted.

"Look Sheriff, I've got cancer and the doc only gives me six months at best to live. I'm sure if you dig deep enough, you can find evidence."

"I've got long brown hair found on Gary's clothes, what was left of them. You don't have long brown hair. You're bald!"

Without missing a beat—probably because he heard Bart and Corny talking about it and the quilt—Emmett produced a long brown wig from his back pocket.

"This belonged to my sister, and I caught Gary going through her things after she died. So, I killed him," Emmett insisted.

"What about the quilt? How do you explain that?" the sheriff demanded.

"I uh. I stole it offun Sarah's clothesline when I was a plottin' to killed him. Come on, Sheriff, just arrest me and let Lucinda go. Let me have this. It's time I fess up to my crimes and clear my conscience," Emmett pleaded. "I always wanted to be a hero in my hometown and I've wanted it for a long time. When I joined the Army in October 1898, I planned to go to the Spanish-American War for my country, but the war was over afer I got there. Then the Army sent me to the Philippines, but I got sent home when I contracted that Dengue fever. When the Great War came, I was too old, and the military didn't want me. Let me do this for my hometown. Let me be the hero for once in my life. I wanted to be like Amos Conaway and those other boys who died for their country and got their names on the plaque at the courthouse, but it just weren't in the cards for me. So let me do this one thing. Gary Green hurt enough folks; no one else needs to suffer by him."

The sheriff looked around at everyone's faces – most were looking down at the ground with some of the women crying. He finally relented, "Oh, all right. They'll hang you for sure, you know."

"Yes, I'm counting on it," Old Man Jones said with a tired smile. "I just need to get someone to take my dog, Rex. He's a good dog. Weren't no trouble for me ever."

Sean O'Casey stepped forward and said, "I'd be honored to take Rex in and give him a good home."

"Thank ya kindly, Sean. All right then, I reckon I'm ready, Sheriff. I'll sign a paper confessing my guilt. You just tell me what you need."

Unlocking the jail cell, the sheriff said, "You can go free, Miss Hawkins. The rest of you need to get out of my office. There isn't room to move around in here. Now, git!" Shaking his head at the recent developments, the sheriff looked at Emmett Jones and said, "Come on over here, you old fool. Let's get you booked." He opened the jail cell door and led him to his desk.

Deloris whispered to Bert and Les to wait for her outside. She wanted to watch each person's face as they solemnly said goodbye to Emmett and left.

Each female gave him a hug with tears in their eyes, even though it was against proper etiquette, and each man shook his hand, looking him straight in the eye. Sarah walked up to Emmett, gave him a big hug, and said, "Thank you."

Oliver escorted Sarah to the door where she stopped and turned to wait for Lucinda, who was the last one to leave. Lucinda gave Emmett a hug and a kiss on the cheek before saying, "You are my hero, and I'll never forget what you did for me."

Emmett rubbed his eyes, holding back a tear, and said, "That means the world to me, Miss Hawkins."

"Thank you," Lucinda said again, giving him another hug and one last look before walking out of the door with her mother. She stopped at the door to tell Deloris thank you, too.

The sheriff looked at Deloris and said resignedly, "Well, don't you have some place to be?"

"Oh, yes." Deloris knew that Old Man Jones didn't really murder Gary Green, and the sheriff knew it too. She looked at Emmett Jones and said, "You're my hero, too." She gave him a hug and slipped out door before tears started rolling down her cheeks.

Outside, more people were arriving and walking down the block to the Sheriff's Office, but Mayor Fine waved them off, saying, "Everything is taken care of. You can all go back to the picnic or go home." He was still there when Les pulled his car away to return to the picnic.

Bert and Les tried to make small talk, but Deloris sat quietly, trying to sort out the recent developments.

CHAPTER 23

The Drawing

Les took Bert and Deloris back to the picnic where about half of the free items had been given away, but there was still more to draw for in the free drawing. Apparently, Mayor Fine put one of the other men in charge of the drawing while he went to the Sheriff's Office in Gallatin, but he took over when he arrived back just behind Deloris, Bert, and Les.

The mayor climbed the steps and stood tall up on the bandstand with a megaphone in hand. "Okay, sorry, folks. I had some town business to tend to, but I'm back now. What do we have next?"

"We have a load of gravel for your driveway," Mrs. Martin called out, reading from a sheet of paper. He repeated what she said into the megaphone.

A child from the audience had been recruited to reach into the bucket and pull out a name. Emmett Jones was the name drawn. Stunned for a moment, Mayor Fine quickly said, "Oh, uhm, Emmett had to leave the picnic early. Let's draw another name." Those in the know lowered their heads.

The child handed another slip of paper to the mayor, who read aloud, "Lara Cogswell."

Lara rose from her chair and said, "I don't know what I'll do with a load of gravel since I live in town."

While most folks in the audience laughed at Lara's comment, Deloris could tell that the joy of the drawing was diminished for those that had just witnessed Emmett Jones' sacrifice. An older child brought Lara the slip of paper with the prize written on it. She accepted it and then turned to Sean O'Casey, seated nearby.

"Oh, I guess you could use the gravel, couldn't you?"

He smiled and nodded as she handed him the paper.

"Our next prize is a sack of flour from Thompson's General Store," Mrs. Martin said, which again the mayor repeated for all to hear.

The child pulled a name and Mayor Fine announced, "Clarence Markham!"

"Clarence Markham," Mayor Fines repeated.

Deloris stood up, hid her hand behind her back and crossed her fingers before saying, "I don't think he can hear you. He's in the back, getting something from his car. I'll accept it for him."

Winners had to be present to receive the prizes, but luckily, they believed Deloris. Technically, he was present and getting a nap in his car, so she didn't lie. He just wasn't in a state to accept his prize. The same child came through the crowd to hand her the paper with that prize written on it, which she put in her purse.

"Next we have a sack of popcorn, processed right here in Jameson at the Evers Popcorn Mill."

"Craig Ness!"

On it went until the last prize was drawn, and Mrs. Penny Powers' name was called. In all of her life, Deloris never had her name called at the picnic and it was always a little disheartening. Just once, she'd like to win a shave at the local barbershop, a sack of flour or a load of gravel—just something. But Clarence had won, and that was as close as she was going to get to winning this year. Maybe she'd have better luck at next year's picnic.

With the drawing over, the crowd dispersed, except for those left to clean up. Deloris ran over to the cookshack and asked if she could get a cup of coffee before they poured it all out. She took it to Clarence still in his car, waking him up and encouraging him to drink it. When he finished, she ran back to the cookshack's kitchen to wash the cup and put it away. Thanking the folks who were still there, she slipped out and hurried through the darkness back to Clarence.

"Do you think you can drive?" she asked him.

"Yeah, I'm okay. I can drive," he said, rubbing his face. "Man, that stuff hit me like a ton of bricks."

"Well, you aren't accustomed to drinking anything that strong," Deloris sympathized.

"Nope," Clarence admitted, and it made Deloris feel better to know that her brother wasn't that accustomed to drinking. "Okay, let's go," he said, taking a deep breath and straightening his shoulders.

"Well, you sure have missed some things," Deloris began as she climbed in the car. On the ride home, she filled him in on the developments, and, remembering the drawing, added, "Oh by the way, there is a sack of flour that belongs to you at Thompsons."

"Huh?"

"They called your name, and I collected the prize for you. I told them you were back in your car getting something. I didn't exactly lie. You were back at your car, getting a nap," she laughed as she showed him the envelope.

"Oh, not so loud," Clarence cautioned with a wince. "I swear that my head is splitting wide open."

At home, the siblings crept upstairs, avoiding the spots on the steps that creaked and could wake any of the sleepers. It was a mission they both had accomplished many times over the years since their parents went to bed early and both Clarence and Deloris liked to stay out late with their friends. Late of course was only eleven p.m. in other households.

As they were on the stairs, there was a rumble of another car out front. They both paused, and when Deloris recognized the voices she smiled. "It's Bert and Roy dropping off Thelma," she whispered to Clarence.

Thelma came inside as quietly as her siblings had and saw them standing on the stairs. All three tried hard not to laugh at their predicament, but they shook with silent chuckles as they carefully climbed the stairs.

"What happened at the Sheriff's Office?" Thelma whispered.

"I'll tell you when we go to bed," Deloris whispered back.

Trying not to wake her nieces in the bed next to them, Deloris told Thelma all about it.

CHAPTER 24
Sunday Dinner

After church Sunday morning, everyone came home to prepare for the Sunday dinner. Everyone also included Mildred and Bereniece. Nannie had baked a ham earlier that morning before the day got hot so that when they got home, all that needed to be done was the fixins to go with it. Nannie heated scalloped potatoes from the day before, and she put Deloris to preparing the apples for frying and had Thelma peel and cut up cucumbers and tomatoes. When Deloris finished with the apples, her mother sent her into the root cellar to get a few jars of green beans she canned the summer before to supplement the fresh beans she picked and snapped yesterday. Deloris' cousin Mildred washed dishes while her sister, Berniece, watched her and Mildred's babies. As more family members arrived, each one was given a task to help complete the meal.

The conversation around the dinner table was about the picnic and Clarence's sharpshooting capabilities. He basked in the accomplishment's glory.

"Where did ya git to, Clarence? I didn't see ya most of the night," Nannie inquired.

"Oh, I was hanging out with some of my friends... we went down to the river and then over to one of their houses."

Clarence wasn't a very good liar, because his face had guilt written all over it, so Deloris piped up and changed the subject to take the focus off him. "Did you hear they arrested Lucinda Hawkins last night?" she asked.

"I didn't hear that," Will said.

Nannie frowned. "Oh dear, that can't be right. I hope she's okay."

"Well, the sheriff released her when Old Man Jones confessed," Deloris added.

"That's Mr. Jones to you," Nannie corrected without registering what Deloris said. Then it hit her, and she asked, "He confessed?"

"Yes, he did, as did half the town."

"What? An' how do you know all this?"

"I, uh, I was at the Sheriff's Office last night when they all came in, including Mr. Jones," Deloris confessed.

"What?" Nannie cried out as she started to choke from the drink of water she just took. "Why were you there?"

"I went to help Lucinda."

In frustration, Nannie threw her napkin down and look squarely at Deloris and then Clarence. "Deloris, you need to be staying out o' their business. Clarence, why'd you take her? You shouldn't have taken her there. I thought I raised you both better'n that."

Before Clarence could reply, Deloris interjected. "Mrs. Gibbs asked me to help Lucinda, and I have been working on the case for her."

Nannie was not impressed. "I don't like that one bit.

PECULIARITIES AT THE PICNIC

Not one bit. Listen here, I still don't approve at all of you getting involved."

"Mother, I am an adult now." Deloris set her fork down and looked her mother in the eye. "I can take care of myself. Look at how I helped Austin when my co-worker was murdered at Poppy's Paradise Park."

"It just ain't right for you to go running all over the place. It's no place for a lady to act like that."

"Your mother is right, Deloris," Will added looking at Nannie and shaking his head.

"I had Bert with me at the Sheriff's Office. Aren't we supposed to help take care of those in need?" Deloris replied. "And I only have one more thing to do. Miss Cogswell asked me to come visit this afternoon. There's no harm in a neighborly visit when I've been invited." Deloris knew her mother's weak spot.

Nannie looked upset as she started wringing her hands, but since she believed in taking care of others and being neighborly, it was hard for her to argue with that, so she finally groaned and said, "You be careful now. You hear?"

"Yes, Momma."

The others around the table remained quiet until this exchange ended. Then Clarence spoke up, "Momma, I won a sack of flour for you last night at the picnic."

Nannie smiled at this revelation, and the conversation moved back to the picnic. When dinner was over, Mildred, Bert, and Thelma helped Nannie clean the kitchen while Berniece watched the babies again. Deloris and Clarence took advantage of everyone being busy to slip out of the house and head to Bethany in his car.

Clarence spoke first, asking, "Do we still need to go to these places today? The sheriff already arrested Old Man Jones. Isn't that good enough for you?"

"No, Clarence, it isn't, because everyone knows he didn't do it," Deloris insisted. If he buried Gary Green under the bandstand, then why didn't he move the body before he started to work on it? He would have known it was there."

"I suppose you have a point," Clarence relented.

"I want the truth, no matter what," Deloris stated as they pulled up to Cathy and Silas Narramore's house outside of Bethany.

CHAPTER 25

The Narramores

Deloris knocked on the Narramores' door and Cathy welcomed her and Clarence inside. Cathy offered them a glass of tea and they all took seats in her living room that was obviously full of hand me down furniture.

Deloris introduced Clarence to them just as someone else came out of the kitchen.

"I invited Cindy here too. I hope you don't mind," Cathy said.

"No, I don't mind. Having you both here will give me a clearer picture of Amos Conaway and I wanted to talk with her after last night anyway." Deloris smiled at Lucinda as Lucinda took a seat. Pulling out her tablet, she turned to the whole group and asked, "So, what kind of person was Amos?"

Silas cleared his throat and spoke up first. "Hey Clarence, do you want to go out to the barn with me? I need a little help with something."

Deloris quickly spoke up. "I have some questions for you, too. I hope you won't mind."

173

"Okay, how about you ask me first?" Silas offered. "I didn't know Amos Conaway very well, but I wouldn't blame him or anyone else for killing Gary Green. Gary was a cheat, a coward, and a liar."

Deloris said, "I've heard that about him. Were you at the picnic the year Cindy left town?"

"No, I was in town in July but left before the picnic which, Cathy tells me, is usually in August. I never went to the picnic until I married Cathy." He shifted in his seat. "Selling the car to Gary, I just chalked up as a learning experience, after someone told me what he did to other people who tried to set things right with him. By the way, you said something about me getting my car back?"

"Was your car the one Gary Green was driving back then?" Clarence interrupted.

"Yes, I guess it was."

"Was it a 1916 Model T?" he asked.

"Yes."

"Then I can help you with that. If you are free this coming Tuesday, I'll take you to your car. Mind you, it is pretty dirty, but otherwise in pretty good shape."

"I don't care about that," Silas said. "I can clean and fix it up. I just want to get it back so that I can sell it and finally get some money out of it. Thanks."

"How about we go see what you need help with in the barn," Clarence offered as he rose from his seat and started walking toward the door.

Silas did the same, but stopped and looked back at Deloris. "Oh, is that all you had for me?" he asked.

"Yes. I don't have any more questions. Thank you," Deloris said as she crossed his name on her list and wrote something on the next page.

With a knowing wink, Deloris said to Cathy and

PECULIARITIES AT THE PICNIC

Lucinda, "Having them out of here is probably better, anyway. We can be more open." They nodded their heads in agreement. Turning toward Lucinda, she started again, "Cindy, I presume you told Cathy what happened last night at the Sheriff's Office?"

"Yes, I did."

Cathy spoke up, "That was crazy how everyone confessed to the murder, but if I had known Cindy had been arrested, I would have been there throwing a fit too, and maybe confessing myself!"

"Lucinda, I mean Cindy, sorry. What did you think of everyone confessing?"

"I certainly didn't expect anything like that to happen. I thought my goose was cooked."

"That shows how much everyone in this town cares about you and they know you didn't do it, but which one of them actually did it?"

"I really don't know." Lucinda's frown deepened.

"Sometimes I wonder if it is really worth it to find out who actually killed Gary Green since he was such a scoundrel," Deloris said. "Then other times, I have a pang of needing to know the truth and seeing justice served. I've always needed to see things through to the end." She shrugged. "So, I continue."

Lucinda nodded. "I kind of want to know too, just so that I can thank them. Heaven knows where I'd be or what would have happened to me if he was still alive and he had found me," she said with a shudder.

Deloris shifted topics. "What kind of person was Amos Conaway?"

"Oh, Amos didn't do it. I am certain of that, but he could have wanted to, since I wrote to him why I left that night," Lucinda responded. "Amos was charming, caring, and protective of me. When I was with him, I felt safe—safe from Gary, safe from worry, and safe from the world." Her eyes filled with tears and her shoulders slumped. Cathy jumped up to comfort her friend.

Sniffing a little, Lucinda continued, "I hated to leave him, most of all. That hurt me more than I realized at the time. I wrote a couple of letters to him, but didn't get a response, so I figured he had moved on."

Writing a note about the letters on her tablet, Deloris went on, "What about you, Cathy? What can you tell me about Amos after Cindy left?"

"Well, as I said last night, he was very upset that Cindy had left," Cathy explained. "Then he left town for about three months, and when he returned, he looked miserable and had lost weight. He seemed vacant, as if he was going through the motions of life, but not really there. He was a gentleman through and through, and losing Cindy almost killed him. He seemed lost without her and never had another girlfriend."

As Lucinda started tearing up again, Cathy put her arm around her. "You know he died in the Great War?" she asked Deloris. "There is a plaque to honor him in front of the courthouse and on the Jameson post office wall. I heard his name might also be somewhere at the new Liberty Memorial in Kansas City."

"I've seen the two plaques, but I didn't know anything about him. I am so sorry to be bringing all of this heartache back to you," Deloris said softly.

"I understand your need to ask," Lucinda said, dabbing at her nose. "I haven't told very many people here, but I am engaged to be married in December. That is another reason I came home. I wanted to tell my mother and Cathy." Taking a deep breath, she continued, "I would have liked to apologize to Amos and see why he never responded to my letters. I must have missed seeing the paper with his death notice in it. Anyway, after I saw in the newspapers that Gary was dead, I knew it was safe to come home."

"Fate played a cruel trick on you," Cathy added.

"Yes, I believe it did," Lucinda replied.

"His death was in the newspapers in St. Louis?" Deloris asked.

"Oh no, I had *The Jameson Gem* mailed to Miss Cogswell's friend's home, and I read it there."

"I see. Well, I believe that is all I wanted to ask everyone. Clarence and I should be going. I'm going to Lara Cogswell's house next. Do you want to go with us, Cindy?"

"I drove here, so I can just follow you there."

"Okay."

The three women walked outside to the barn, where they found the fellows chatting away about the best twine to bundle up hay.

"We're ready to go," Deloris told Clarence.

"We?"

"Yes, Cindy is going to follow us there."

"I see."

When Deloris, Clarence and then Cindy pulled up in front of Lara Cogswell's house, they could see several people were inside. Deloris was glad that Lucinda was with her as they walked to the front door. Hopefully, with Lucinda there, she could finally get to the truth of what had happened fourteen years ago. Clarence opened the door and held it for the two women. Everyone from the night before except for Emmett Jones was there, making small talk that stopped as soon as they saw Clarence, Deloris, and Lucinda.

"Oh, Lucinda. I am so glad that you are here," Lara said.

"I tried to call you, but your mother said you left and she didn't know where you went or when you'd be back. I invited her today, too."

Sarah Gibbs stepped out from the crowd in the dining room and walked over to give her daughter a hug.

Lara turned to face Deloris and said, "You deserve to know the truth. Last night after I saw everyone confess, I knew that we all needed to sort this out to put this horrible experience behind us once and for all. We are here to trying to piece everything together and figure it out ourselves."

Deloris said, "I appreciate you including me and allowing me this opportunity to learn the truth. I promise that whatever is said here will not be divulged by me or my brother to the sheriff," Deloris said as she made a sweeping gesture toward Clarence.

"I know nothing and I see nothing. Your secrets are safe with me," Clarence said with a motion of zipping his mouth, as he took a seat in the back of the dining room to observe Deloris going to work.

CHAPTER 26

Town Meeting

Deloris sat down and took out her tablet and pencil, poised to write anything down that might be important. "Please proceed," she said.

To Deloris' surprise, Nellie Robertson stepped forward and said, "First, I just want to say that I am sorry for the way we treated you when you were asking questions. We were afraid of what you would do if you found out the truth, and that you would tell the sheriff."

"Yes, when we heard that you work for the Kansas City Police Department," Moira Harvey chimed in, "we decided to avoid talking to you altogether."

"Oh, that." Deloris felt a little sheepish. "I work for the switchboard at the police department. I'm not a detective. I said that to get people to talk to me, but it didn't help, obviously. I did help solve a murder in the city a few months ago, but ..."

A collective sigh, followed by a gasp, came from several attendees as Deloris divulged this information. She stopped there because it wasn't helping her to learn the truth from them, and switched back to questioning them. Maybe, finally, she'd get some answers now.

With a wave of her hand, she went on, "I don't want to talk about that. I want to know what happened here fourteen years ago. From what I have learned about Gary Green, this will probably be considered a case of justifiable homicide. If you don't want me to tell the sheriff, I won't. Are you still willing to tell me the truth now?" Deloris asked.

Standing in a corner, Lara nodded, stepped forward and spoke up a little nervous at first. "Yes. It was just after the picnic in 1917, when Lucinda, in her nightgown and wrapped in a quilt, came running to my door and started banging on it in a fit of fright. I let her in, and she told me that Gary Green attacked her in a drunken stupor. I halfway expected this to happen, because, you see, Gary attacked and had his way with me when we were in high school."

There was a moment of stunned silence from everyone in the room at this revelation. Lara cleared her throat and continued, "I never wanted to talk about it or think about it until now. I guess it affected me more than I cared to admit. I withdrew from all my friends and the boy I cared for the most."

Lara glanced at Sean O'Casey nervously, her cheeks reddening with shame. He walked over and took her hand and kissed it. Then he put his arm around her shoulders still holding her hand. No one had ever seen such tenderness from him before, and they were dumbfounded at this new, gentle man.

"And I never understood why she withdrew. It made me angry at the world that she had snubbed me and never accepted my invitations," Sean said, still holding Lara's hand.

With strengthened resolve, Lara continued, "Lucinda had come to me before, upset about something Gary had said or done, and of course I believed her, but there really wasn't anything I could do to protect her until she was ready to leave. She didn't want to leave her mother, and I understood that. So, I watched for any signs that he was abusing her."

Sarah started crying softly, "I, I should have known that he'd try something like that with Cindy. I wanted to get her away from him, but I felt like we were both trapped. He controlled all of our money and I didn't know where to turn."

"I know, dear," Maude said soothingly to Sarah. "He was a real smooth talker when he wanted to be and fooled the lot of us at one time or another. I just wish you had come to us for help before any of this happened."

"But what could you have done?" Sarah asked. "Everyone was afraid of him."

"Not my Tom," Maude said proudly. "But we could have at least gotten Lucinda out earlier, and found a safe place for you, as well."

Lara picked up her story again. "I talked with a friend of mine in St Louis in advance and arranged for Lucinda to stay with her and help her get a job, just in case something ever happened. I kept a bag packed and ready with some clothes that I thought would fit Lucinda. I had already drilled some holes in a large steamer trunk for Lucinda to hide in and be able to breathe if I needed to get her out of town unseen. The night that Lucinda knocked, I'd already been planning on traveling to the Missouri State Teacher Association convention, so it couldn't have worked out better. I'm just glad that I was still home. We loaded up the steamer trunk in the rumble seat and I had Lucinda get in. Then I put the top shelf in the trunk and piled a bunch of books on top of the shelf. Instead of leaving early the next morning for the train station like I'd planned, I just left that evening with Lucinda. Before we left, I ran out the back door to Maude's house to tell her I was going out of town early and asked if she would keep an eye on my house. When Lucinda and I left that night for Gallatin, as I was pulling out, I saw Gary running down the street, so I sped out of town as fast as I could."

Sean O'Casey shook his head and interjected, "Lara, I suspect you saw me coming down the street instead of Gary."

Lara gasped, but Sean took her hand again and continued, "I saw Lucinda run by my house and she dropped something. I ran out to pick it up, intending to return it to her, and to find out why she was running into town. That must have been when you saw me. When I saw it was a man's pocket watch, I stopped. Gary often bragged about the watch that he inherited from his father, and I recognized this watch as his. In the distance, I saw Gary running, weaving all over the road and falling down, then getting up and running some more. That's when I decided to hide behind some shrubbery and watch him. I figured Lucinda must have been running from him. I was prepared to take him out of this world if he hurt either of you."

"Oh, I see," Lara smiled at Sean. Then she continued. "I rented a room at the hotel in Gallatin and slipped Lucinda in when no one was looking. Early the next morning, I bought two tickets on the train for St. Louis and we left. After we boarded the train and it started to move, I went to the baggage car and waited until the porter left and no one else was around. Then I opened the trunk and took the books and shelf out of it so Lucinda could step out of it. I handed her a ticket and we went to our seats. I took her to my friend in St. Louis, went to my conference, and returned to Jameson one week later. Neither Sarah, Maude, Moira, nor Nellie knew anything about my plan because I didn't want them to slip up and say something that could get back to Gary." She looked at her friends apologetically. "I told Lucinda to mail me a letter for her mother and a quick note to me signed Grasshopper, just to let me know she was settled in. After that, she was to only write to me if something was wrong by sending a note through my friend at her work. I was afraid Gary would find her and I couldn't take a chance of that happening."

"How did it go from helping Lucinda to get out of town to murdering Gary and burying his body under the bandstand?" Deloris asked.

"Let me take it from here, dear," Maude broke in. "After Lara left, I heard a loud commotion when Gary arrived at her house. He was banging on her back door, then he ran to the front and started banging on that door. I peeked out of my back door and could hear him yelling obscenities. He was threatening to teach her a lesson like he did when they were in school."

At this, Lara hung her head in shame again, but Sean put his hand under her chin to look her in the eyes. "It's okay. He is gone for good now and can't hurt anyone anymore." Lara nodded.

"When he didn't get a response," Maud continued, "he started running around the house, threatening to kill both Lara and Lucinda if he got his hands on them."

Then Nellie added, "He was banging on the doors and windows causing quite a ruckus. He would have awoken half the town, but most folks, including my husband, were at a Knights of Pythias meeting to recap the picnic. I'd skipped it because I had a headache."

"And Tom and I didn't attend because we were leaving on the early train the following morning. We needed to be up at five," Maude explained.

"Only Maude and I were close enough to hear what he was saying," Nellie continued. "Anyone who lived further away would have simply thought it was a drunk making noise."

"Including me, but not my husband." Maude mused for a minute, looking at Tom. "No, not him. Once he's asleep, nothing can wake him up. I always said that a team of wild horses could run me over lying in the bed next to him and he wouldn't wake up."

It was Tom's turn to look a little sheepish, shrugging as a blush creeping onto his cheeks.

Nellie continued, "I peeked out of my window to see what was happening. Then I saw Gary grab the ladder that Emmett left leaning against my house when he was there the day before repairing a window. I didn't see Lara leave, and I was afraid that she was inside. When I saw Lara had the attic window open to vent the sultry summer air, I assume he planned to climb the ladder to crawl into that window and gain access to her house. He must have missed an upper rung on the ladder because he fell off and it knocked him unconscious for a minute or two, or maybe he just passed out because he was obviously drunk and slurring his speech. Either way, I went running out of the house and grabbed my shovel that was leaning against the porch and—"

"—No, dear. Let me interrupt," Maude said gently. "It was my shovel. I brought it with me when I heard and then saw the commotion. Just a few minutes earlier Lara had run to my back door and told me she was leaving. When I heard him yell that he was going to attack Lara and even kill her, well, I guess I lost it." She sighed. "You see, Gary tried to attack me once, too. I stood over him and when I saw him start to get up after that fall off the ladder, I hit him in the head with my shovel. The next thing I knew, I was hitting him again and again with the shovel."

"Oh, then I grabbed my rolling pin," Nellie said remembering. "It's all a bit jumbled in my head. I was so terrified. He grabbed my hair, and I hit him again and again. Somehow, I tore my hair loose from his grasp. I started kicking him and hitting him with my rolling pin some more, and Maude was hitting him with the shovel. All those years of pent-up emotion and fear just took us over, I guess. Before we realized what we were doing, he was dead," she said, her voice wavering with emotion.

Maude added, "You see, my daughter was twelve years old then and Nellie's daughter was eleven. I didn't want him trying anything with either girl. Or with any girl or woman in town and beyond, for that matter. I guess that I just went momentarily insane."

Nellie, on the verge of tears, added, "He had his way with me, too, when we were teenagers. My mother and father were both in Gallatin and I was home alone. He never let me forget it."

Nellie and Maude's husbands both had looks like they could kill Gary again, right then and there, if he wasn't already dead.

"As I was saying," Maude picked up again, "I didn't want him hurting my daughter or anyone's daughter. I wanted him gone forever. He attempted to attack me once as well, but Tom and I were dating then and Tom intimidated Gary. You see, Tom is taller and stronger than Gary was, and Tom intimidates folks with his size." She paused to smile at her husband before continuing with the story.

"Well, while Nellie ran to her shed to get a wheelbarrow, I stood over him with the shovel. Then, when she returned, I went looking for something to cover him up, while she stood over him with the shovel in case he came to. I found a quilt laying on the ground in Lara's yard and covered him up with it. I guess it belonged to Lucinda. We struggled to get Gary's body into the wheelbarrow, but we managed. Then we pushed it half a block, but with the recent rains it was impossible to push it much farther through the mud. Let me tell you, that was harder than we thought it would be. We talked about burying his body in the line of trees at the edge of the picnic grounds."

Nellie interrupted, "So, I ran home to see if Owen was back from the Pythias dinner yet and could help us with the wheelbarrow, and he had come home to check on me. And Maude ran home to see if she could wake Tom up. Maude took Tom's hand and looked lovingly at him. We explained to our husbands what had happened, and that we were afraid of what Gary would do to us, if he wasn't dead and awoke. We were only gone for maybe ten minutes."

Maude continued, "Even though it didn't take long to tell everything to Tom and Owen and bring them to help, when we returned, the wheelbarrow was gone, and we assumed Gary wasn't dead. We thought he came to and took the wheelbarrow. We searched and searched that night for him and the wheelbarrow. We were so scared of what he would do to us the next day." Maude shuddered, and Tom put his arm around her.

After a moment to let the experience sink in, Deloris encouraged quietly, "Please continue."

PECULIARITIES AT THE PICNIC

Sean, who had listened quietly to Nellie and Maude tell their story, stood up and said, "I guess this is where I need to tell my part of the story. When I heard what he was shouting about attacking Lara, I started to come out from behind the bushes. I didn't know what I was going to do to him, or how, but I would not let Gary hurt anyone. I stood up, then I saw Nellie and Maude attacking him. I saw the events unfold, exactly as Nellie and Maude told you."

He cleared his throat and continued, "When I saw them struggling to push the wheelbarrow down the street toward the picnic grounds, I was going to come out of hiding and offer to help them, but then they both left. I didn't know what they had planned to do with Gary, but I could see that he was dead or dying. I slipped over there and pushed the wheelbarrow down the block to the picnic grounds myself. I thought it would be best if they didn't know what happened to him, thinking that he got up and ran away—not knowing if they killed him or not."

"I pushed the wheelbarrow with Gary's body to my barn and hid it there while I collected a shovel, a hammer, some nails and another board. I thought it would be best to bury the body under the bandstand where wild animals couldn't reach it and drag it out to be exposed. When all the other townsfolk went home after the Knights of Pythias' meeting and Maude, Tom, Nellie, and Owen gave up searching, I still had a few hours of darkness left. I dragged Gary's body back to the park, where I pried off some boards around the bottom of the bandstand and dug a hole under it. I placed him in the hole and threw his watch on top of him. When I finished burying the body, I nailed the boards back and added an extra board to make sure the space was covered with no gaps for any animals to get inside. I then put the wheelbarrow in my barn and went home. After a few days, I left the wheelbarrow in front of Owen and Nellie's house late one night." When he finished talking, he returned back to stand beside Lara.

"Well, that explains how we got the wheelbarrow back," Nellie said, looking up at Sean. "It sure scared me. We didn't know what happened to him or the wheelbarrow. We certainly didn't intend to murder him. It just sort of... happened... but we weren't sure if he was dead or alive."

"I guess that I should have told you," he said apologetically, but I thought at the time that I was helping you. When I saw the bandstand was destroyed in the tornado, I thought I had the body buried deep enough that it would still be hidden. It would have been fine except for Emmett's dern dog. Well, my dern dog..."

Moira stepped in to add, "Nellie and Maude told me what happened when the body was found, and I've been hosting them and Lara at my shop to talk about it and try to figure things out. I'm sorry if we were rude to you, Deloris, but we really didn't want anyone digging up what happened. We weren't even sure what happened ourselves," she explained, raising her shoulders.

"That's quite all right," Deloris replied.

Lara broke in with another question: "So, what happened to Gary's car? I was surprised that he didn't come after me in it."

Clarence, who had been listening intently as everyone told their stories, stood up from the back of the room and said, "I can answer that." And then he told them about Clifford stealing Gary's car and hiding it. It was his way of getting even with Gary for having hit him that afternoon and calling him names.

Sarah spoke up then, saying, "I want to thank all of you

for helping Lucinda. I don't know what would have happened to her if you hadn't."

Lucinda, with tears in her eyes, said, "Thank you all very much for coming forward with your stories and especially thank you everyone for what you did last night at the jail. Miss Cogswell, I've been waiting fourteen years to tell you thank you for getting me away from Gary."

The room went silent for a moment.

Swallowing hard, Lara broke the silence. "Well, I didn't know what was happening with Gary, but I knew I needed to get you out of town and on the train to St. Louis. I didn't come back for a week, so, you see, neither Lucinda nor I knew what happened to Gary after that night. We just thought that he was still out there looking for her, so she stayed hidden. Then, when his body was discovered, Nellie and Maude finally told me their story at Moira's shop." Looking at Lucinda, she added, "They thought I should know what happened when you started asking questions."

"Yes, that's true. I didn't know what happened to Gary that night," Lucinda confirmed. "As soon as I found out, I came home to see my mother."

Deloris stood and said, "Thank you all for telling me your stories, no matter how painful they were. It looks like Emmett will be the hero he always wanted to be."

Everyone nodded their agreement.

Then Lucinda stood up and said, "To end this on a happier note, you are all invited to my wedding this December here in Jameson."

"December!" Nellie said. "Remember, northwest Missouri winters can be brutal."

"I remember," Lucinda said and smiled, "but I don't think a little weather is going to slow down this group.

"Who's the lucky guy?" Tom Fine asked.

"I met him in St. Louis. He plans to come for a visit next weekend and meet my mother. I will introduce him to all of you, too."

"Well, you'd better. We need to decide if he is good enough for you," Tom said sternly, but with a smile on his face.

One by one, they each wished her well and surrounded her in a circle of love and support.

Then Deloris and Clarence arose and quietly exited. As they drove home, they discussed the stories they had just heard and the support they just witnessed.

"I think you did the right thing," Clarence said reassuringly.

"I hope so," Deloris replied, but having Emmett take the blame still nagged at her.

When Austin came to pick up Thelma and the girls to go back to the city, Deloris told him thank you, but she had decided to go back on the train. She didn't tell him she wanted time to reflect on the weekend, and knew she wouldn't have that chance sitting with the girls. Clarence would take her to the train station.

Epilogue
ENDINGS AND BEGINNINGS

Sometimes, you just need to walk away and leave well enough alone. It was a hard pill to swallow for Deloris, knowing the wrong person was being charged for Gary Green's murder, but she felt it was for the best. While she usually believed that no one deserved to be murdered, people were much happier now that they were certain Gary Green wouldn't come back to harass and harm them. It wasn't a murder that she'd solved, anyway, but more a case of self-defense. While fighting with this dilemma, she had an inspiration.

When Clarence dropped Deloris off at the station on Sunday for her return to Kansas City, she discovered she was on the same train as Les Wells, who bought her a grape Polly's Pop in the dining car and kept her company all the way back.

"I thought you had a car?" Deloris asked.

"Oh, that car belonged to my aunt," he said, laughing. "I just borrowed it to go to the picnic."

By the time the train arrived at the Kansas City station,

Les had her phone number and she'd agreed to go out to the movies with him the next weekend.

When she went to work at the police station the next morning, she told Austin everything and asked him what she should do. Technically, she was keeping her promise by not telling the sheriff, and she knew Austin would understand better than anyone else. He listened intently to her story, but he didn't take notes, which seemed uncharacteristic for him. When she finished, a few tears formed in her eyes, and he did something else unusual and gave her a hug. He told her that he would take care of it and for her not to worry about it, putting her mind at ease.

Deloris never did see or hear anything more about it. Everyone else apparently moved on and she felt that she could now move on too.

Lara Cogswell wrote Deloris a month after the picnic and told her that she and Sean O'Casey had been married by the Justice of the Peace in Gallatin. Now they could finally start their lives over with a chance to be happy together. Because Lara had a bigger, nicer house that she had inherited from her parents when they passed, Sean moved into her house and let Liam move into his house.

Alfie wrote, too, telling Deloris that Liam had met someone else. She had spotted him with someone new at Ma Robbins' place, buying hamburgers and sharing a milkshake. It was news that she was more than happy to pass on to Deloris.

Lucinda did get married in Jameson that December, and most of the town attended, even Deloris and her family. In fact, Lucinda's wedding was one of the largest weddings ever held at the Christian Church. She and her groom returned to St. Louis after a honeymoon at the Lake of the

Ozarks with many promises to come back to Jameson for frequent visits with her mother and stepfather.

Emmett Jones died peacefully two months after his arrest but before his case went to court for the murder of Gary Green. Though he'd been kept in jail, not a day went by without multiple visitors from Jameson bearing all kinds of food and desserts. The sheriff grumbled that his jail was becoming a parlor, but never too loudly, because he too enjoyed eating the baked goods brought to the jail.

After Emmett's death, a plaque was placed in front of the new bandstand in his honor:

THIS BANDSTAND IS DEDICATED TO THE MEMORY OF
A GREAT MAN, A BRAVE MAN, OUR HERO
EMMETT MERRIWEATHER JONES
BY DECREE OF MAYOR TOM FINE, NOVEMBER 1, 1931

About the Author(s)

Through conversation and stories, two friends who like old movies, mysteries and history started talking about writing a book that featured these elements. One friend has two books published about her mother, Doris Markham. Doris, who lived in Kansas City in the 1930s, experienced some of the stories told in this book. The other friend thought that a detective inspired by Doris Markham would be a great place to begin this writing adventure. As time progressed, the friends developed the Miss Markham Mystery Series. The main character—much like her real-life inspiration—is spunky, hard-headed and fearless. This is the first book of the series; many more of The Miss Markham Mysteries are in the works. The name Juliet E. Sidonie is a combination of the two authors' grandmother's and great-grandmother's names. For more historical content and additional information, visit their website: MissMarkhamMysteries.com.

Additional information for this book may also be found on the website.

Miss Markham Mysteries

BOOK THREE

∼

KILLING THE KANSAS CITY SHUFFLE

∼

Back in Kansas City, how does Deloris' new job at an Italian restaurant go, and why is Sam hiding out from the Mafia?

Join Deloris in her next adventure of love, murder, and the Kansas City Shuffle in Book Three of the Miss Markham Mystery series.

Turn the page to read the prologue.

Prologue

SLICK SAM

Sam Sloan, or Slick Sam, as his friends called him, was a conman. His father was a conman. His grandfather was a conman, and so on down the line; he came by his skills naturally. Finding a mark in 1931 was easy because people were hurting financially, even the rich ones, and they were desperate to make an easy buck anywhere they could.

Sam was at his usual haunt, an Italian restaurant in Kansas City, Missouri, on Grand Avenue, looking for his next mark. He always studied his victims carefully before engaging them in the scam, or the game, as he liked to call it. He knew their likes, their dislikes, their passions, and their shortcomings as well as he knew his own.

As he sat at his favorite table in the back near the kitchen, reading the newspaper and sipping his coffee, the waitress came by.

"Would you like for me to freshen that up for you?"

Sam looked up into the young woman's violet eyes and almost lost himself in their depths. He had never seen violet eyes before. Recovering quickly, he pushed his coffee cup closer to her and said, "Sure, doll. I haven't seen you here before. Did you just step out of my dreams?"

She smiled cautiously as she poured the steaming black liquid into his cup. "I just started working here yesterday. Are you ready to order?"

"How's about you and me getting better acquainted tonight, doll?" he asked, looking her up and down. "I got two tickets to the Pla-Mor's formal reopening tomorrow night. We can dance the night away. Whaddaya say?"

"No thanks," Deloris Markham replied, keeping her eyes on the now-full coffee mug.

"Ah, come on, sugar. Don't be so quick to say no. You really don't want to pass up this once-in-a-lifetime opportunity, do you?" Sam pleaded. "I can be very entertaining."

"I'm sure you can. Did you plan to order something?" Deloris persisted with her order pad and pencil in hand.

"Nah, I just come here for the coffee and the scenery," he said, winking. "How about tomorrow night?"

"Save it, Joe. I already have a boyfriend and we have plans." He didn't need to know that she actually had two boyfriends, because he might take that as an invitation for him to be number three.

"Too bad, and my name is Sam. Sam Sloan. Not Joe. How about you ditch him and go with me? I could show you a real good time."

"Oh, I'm sure you could," Deloris tossed the comment over her shoulder as she walked away to greet the patrons at a table near the front of the restaurant.

Sam watched her walk away until his attention was drawn to the couple who had just walked in. There he was, the man Sam waited to see, standing across the room from him at the door. Julius T. Stockton III was the heir apparent to a lumber tycoon. On his arm was one of the most beautiful women Sam had ever seen: a blonde bombshell who reminded him of Jean Harlow from the movie picture show. He wanted to know her name. No, he reasoned, he had to be careful. Beautiful women were his passion—his downfall. Every time he tried to hook up with one, he wound up on the losing end of the relationship. Married twice and divorced twice, Sam didn't have a penny to his name after being taken to the cleaners when the wives were finished with him. That is why he had to step-up his game picking higher-end chumps.

He first heard about Julius Stockton or Jules, as his friends called him, when Sam read about him winning a tidy sum of money at the Riverside Racetrack. From that information, he knew Jules liked to gamble, making him an easy mark. Jules was close friends with Johnny Lazia, and the two hung out at the Riverside Park Jockey Club's Racetrack. They were more like brothers than friends, really. Sam kept a little black book where he recorded information on all of his marks, and he had gone to the library to read what he could about Jules' life in past issues of the newspapers. Since he was considered one of Kansas City's elite, finding him in the newspapers was easy. His father was often found in pictures rubbing elbows with E.F. Swinney, President of the First National Bank, and R.A. Long, a successful lumberman.

The news press was there to capture every minute of Jules' life, too. He graduated from Pembroke School and was an avid polo and lacrosse player. Jules went to Harvard and majored in business, and his parents were so proud that they threw him a large party to celebrate his return home at the Riverside Park Jockey Club. Since the party, he seldom appeared in the newspapers—just a mention here or there when he attended some girl's soiree or an event at the jockey club. So now, Sam had to put on his investigative hat and dig for more information. He had a buddy, Ronnie the Runt, who worked as a busboy at the Riverside Park Club. He would see what information the Runt could gather and give him a 5% cut of the take from the game. Ronnie had come through, telling Sam that he overheard Jules talking about coming to the Venetian Gardens Restaurant tonight.

Snapping back to reality, Sam quickly put the newspaper up to his face and pretended to be reading it. He wasn't ready to introduce himself to Julius. Soon the time would be right and he'd make his move, but right now he'd watch and learn.

However, this woman was a fresh development. Was Jules' girl making eyes at Sam behind her boyfriend's back? Sam wondered, looking up from his newspaper. Here she was, a knock-out and out of his league, but how could he resist, he reasoned. Sam smiled at her and nodded in recognition of her attention. She smiled back with a slight nod of her own. Oh boy, am I in trouble? He gulped and watched her closely. She seemed to steal a glance at him every chance she got. He had to know her and why she was flirting with him, so he followed them when they left the restaurant against his better judgement.

Check out the next book in the Miss Markham Mysteries, *Killing the Kansas City Shuffle*, to see what happens next.

Made in the USA
Middletown, DE
15 May 2025